The Indian
RESURRECTION

The Indian
RESURRECTION

Sukhdeepak Malvai

PARTRIDGE

To order additional copies of this book, contact
Partridge India
000 800 10062 62
orders.india@partridgepublishing.com

www.partridgepublishing.com/india

CONTENTS

Chapter 1   It Begins 1

Chapter 2   The Investigation Begins 6

Chapter 3   The Dreams..9

Chapter 4   The Guardians 14

Chapter 5   The Scouts 21

Chapter 6   It Escalates...25

Chapter 7   The Movement...29

Chapter 8   Developments 35

Chapter 9   The Landings 41

Chapter 10   Ambitions 51

Chapter 11   The wedding...60

Chapter 12   The Zotharians 65

Chapter 13   More from the Masters....................................70

Chapter 14   War...75

Chapter 15   Challenges..84

Chapter 16   Consolidation 90

Chapter 17   Growth...95

Chapter 18   The Clash...100

Chapter 19   Understanding......................................108
Chapter 20   The Space Pilot................................... 114
Chapter 21   Preparations..122
Chapter 22   The World Comes Together 130
Chapter 23   War With The Invaders 136
Chapter 24   Fear Unites..144
Chapter 25   The Wait.. 151
Chapter 26   The Aliens on Earth 163
Chapter 27   The Shiva Squad...................................166
Chapter 28   The Fight For Survival 172
Chapter 29   The Invasion Fleet................................186
Chapter 30   Zothar Invasion 189

ACKNOWLEDGEMENTS

This book would not have been completed without the encouragement and support of my wife Farida. I am very grateful to her for believing in me and supporting me.

My gratitude also goes out to my son Manav for the cover design.

CHAPTER 1

It Begins

Dawn was breaking as I eased my car into the parking slot.

The drizzle the night before had left puddles on the cemented road.

I stood there facing the wall in front and the graffiti on it. Most of it in Hindi that he could not read but there were pictures like a comic strip on the wall and I tried to figure out what they said.

There was pin drop silence and the absence of the usual early morning sounds intrigued me. I looked around and saw no one and moved towards a doorway recessed in the wall. The door was slightly open so I pushed it and went in to see a flight of narrow stairs in front of me. There was water dripping down, it had a greenish colour and seemed sticky. I quietly crept up the stairs and soon was on the first landing. There was a black door in front of me and since it was ajar, I went in and the stench made me gag. Putting a handkerchief on my nose I went forward and saw that the place was in shambles, papers and other belongings were strewn all over and there were many banknotes scattered all over.

I moved forward slowly and entered the next room; it was empty, no furniture, nothing except something in the centre of the room covered with a blanket. I moved the blanket aside and could see what the reason for the stink was. It was the misshapen mass of what looked like flesh with some green stuff oozing out. The mass was moving slowly, trying to creep forward.

I moved back towards the wall and found a light switch and snapped on the light and looked at the mass again; it appeared jelly-like and glistened in the light and was leaking the green fluid from a small hole in the bottom near the floor. The light was causing some agitation and the mass started to pulse and vibrate. It changed colour and became more substantial. There was a sound like the sound of breathing and the shape changed to that of a young woman who lay on the ground looking at him with vacant eyes. I rubbed my eyes in disbelief and said "Are you alright?" There was no sound from the "woman", she just lay there looking at him and after a while stood up and looked around. "Where am I?" She said. "Mumbai", I said. There was silence and she stood there just staring at me. "Who are you? And what happened here?" I asked. I wondered who had called me and directed me to this place; I was expecting the worst and here was this strange scene that had me puzzled.

She looked at me wordlessly and started to cry. "I was in Delhi last night and don't know what happened to me and how I woke up here," she said.

I noticed that the smell had vanished and so had all the greenish stuff. I asked, "What happened to you?" She looked dazed and shook her head and said, "Do you have a mobile phone? I need to talk to my parents." I just passed my cell to her and looked on as she punched a number. She started talking in Punjabi, as soon as she got a connection and talked she became more alert and aware of her surroundings.

"What is your name?", I asked as she started to sob. "Mansi" she said looking at me with her big round eyes. "Who are you?", she asked. "I am a police officer; I got a call asking me to come here". I was wondering what to do next when she told me she was hungry so I decided to take her out of this depressing place. I took one last look around for clues about what had brought her here but could not find anything at all. There was no trace of the green – sticky substance.

I took her down to my car and we drove in silence until I came to a well-lit area. I spotted a café and stopped outside it. Mansi staggered out of the car; she seemed feeble.

Inside we ordered a bottle or water and coffee and a sandwich for her. She seemed frightened and kept staring at me. I asked her to tell me what happened but she appeared to have no recollection of what had happened to her. I drove her to a hospital and the doctor pronounced that there was nothing wrong with her physically.

I called my senior officer for instructions and was instructed to keep her safe until her relatives arranged for her to go home. I drove her to a hotel but she was not willing to stay there as she did not want to be alone. I arranged for a woman officer to come and in the meantime sat with her in the lobby.

She suddenly wanted to talk and started telling me all about herself and her family. Her father ran a big business and she was the only child, a management graduate who had been working for an MNC for the last seven years. She was a person with few friends and her life was routine. Her last memory was of sitting in her office in Delhi, getting ready to go home. She was puzzled about what had happened to her and relieved that she was unharmed, her purse was intact and nothing was missing from it.

As soon as the woman officer came I took my leave after handing over my card to her. The next day the local office of her company arranged for her to return home. I filed a report and tried to forget all about it. It was the year 1998 and after three years in the Indian Police Service this was the first interesting case that had come my way and it was hard to put it out of my mind.

A few weeks passed and I got a call from her, she just thanked me and told me that she was well. There was a tremor in her voice as she spoke to me and I asked her if everything was alright. There was silence at her end and then she started to cry and said that she was having these strange dreams in which she saw herself waking up in the same place in Mumbai. I just listened to her and wondered what I could do about it. But as she went on she said something that caught my attention. She mentioned the green slime and that she would find small traces of it on her bed in the morning and these would disappear after some time. Delhi was way out of my jurisdiction so I put this whole affair out of my mind.

Two months later I was again directed to a lonely spot where another young lady found in a dazed condition and the officer who found her reported seeing a green slime at that spot.

My boss informed me that there had been many cases reported all over the country and we were being asked to cooperate.

All this was very strange and no one had any idea about the course of action.

I was appointed as the head of this investigation because I was the only one with a science post graduate degree. I was not keen to take this on because I had no idea how to go about tackling this case but my curiosity prevented me from making an excuse to decline it.

CHAPTER 2

The Investigation Begins

I decided to start by speaking to each one of the girls who had been through this strange experience.

There were 11 of them and I talked to all of them. It took me a month to travel and meet all of them.

They were from all over India, all from different states. I first looked at what was common to them. They were all in the age group of 22 to 27, all of them worked for real big firms and spoke English and Hindi and the language of the place their home state. There was one from Gujarat, one from Tamil Nadu, one from Bengal, one from Punjab, one from Delhi, one from Uttar Pradesh, two from Mumbai, and two from Bangalore and one from Kerala. All of them had no recollection of what happened, all of them were in their office and then suddenly found themselves in a strange place very far from where they were. There was, in their recollection, a gap of around 24 hours before they found themselves in a strange new place. All of them were alone in their office. All of them were from similar educational backgrounds. None of them was married or had a boyfriend. Their family backgrounds were quite dissimilar. None of them had any drug or alcohol problem. Their seniors and colleagues highly regarded all of them. They had not met any strangers. The only people they had interacted with were family or co-workers. None of them had got any letters or emails that could offer any clue. Every one of them reported traces of the green slime on their bed or clothes. I floated an inquiry to Interpol to find out about cases like this in any other country and concluded that no such case had been reported so far. Medical examinations of the girls showed nothing abnormal.

I believe in the power of many minds working together so I put together a diverse group of people and we did a brainstorming session. The only useful idea that came out was to arrange for all the girls to be put in a hypnotic state and find out if they could recall something.

The result was a lot of travel for me and the hypnotherapist. We did sessions with all the girls, and all of them could only remember seeing a dazzling flash of light and nothing else until they woke up in a strange place.

During this period two other cases were reported, one from Assam where a girl from Hyderabad "appeared" and another from Amritsar where a girl from Surat showed up.

The pressure from my bosses was building up because the press had got wind of this mystery and the public was clamouring for answers. One good thing was that all the girls were unharmed. I did not get permission to keep them all under observation. There was no clue to follow and I wondered if I should give up.

There were many questions in my mind. Why had only girls been abducted? Why only from India? What was the motive of these "temporary" abductions? Who or what was behind this?

There were no answers so far. I decided to take a few days off and relax my mind. I decided to do what I usually did to clear my mind; I went for a ten day Vipassana camp. The ten days of solitude and silence may give me some answers, I thought.

CHAPTER 3

The Dreams

The Vipassana camp began, and I got into the routine there. I was coming here for the third time, and I had never been so restless before this. Sitting in silence used to be so soothing but this time, I could not let go of my thoughts. Again and again, my mind went to the image of the green slime and the foul smell that accompanied it. After two days of wrestling with my restlessness, I was finally able to surrender to the practice and my mind quietened down. The routine required us to go to bed early and on the third day, as usual, I went to my cottage and went to sleep.

As soon as I slept I was transported to a strange place. There was brilliant moonlight, and there was a mist all around. It was silent, so quiet that it felt unnatural. There was no sound at all. There were trees all around, and I was on a path that went through them. I started walking, and my feet did not make a sound. I felt very peaceful, and I did not have any fearful thoughts, which was unusual under the circumstances. When

I looked up, I could see that the stars were brilliant and were clearer than I had ever seen.

I kept walking for a long time, and I started wondering where I was going. There was nothing but the trees and the path ahead. Strangely, I was not feeling tired even after walking for so long. So I kept walking. Something was drawing me forward; I did not want to sit down. I looked back, again and again, to see if there was anybody behind me but could see nothing but mist. It was strange that when I looked back, I could see only a few feet ahead, but when I looked ahead, I could see far ahead. It was as though the mist was denser behind me.

I heard a bell ring and woke up. It was 3 am and time for the next day routine. Getting through my morning ablutions, I wondered about the strange dream and what it meant. I decided to focus on the daily meditation practice. But my thoughts kept wandering back to the dream and the girls and their strange experience. It took me a long time to settle down and sort out my mind and meditate as required.

The day came to an end, and I went back to sleep and was back on the path again. Everything was the same. I started walking faster hoping to reach somewhere soon. The road stretched ahead endlessly and everything was the same. There were the same trees on both sides. The path kept going straight ahead. After a long time I could see a difference, the path ahead was curving to the right. I speeded up to see what lay beyond the curve. As I went forward to the point where the road curved, I saw a structure far ahead. It was too far to see what it was. I kept walking, and it just would not get near. Perhaps it is too far ahead, I thought.

I heard the bell ring again, and I awoke from my dream. It was the first time I had the same dream again and that too with continuity. I decided to see what would happen next and kept to the routine of the day. The vision kept disturbing my practice, and I had to fight to keep my sleep and my "dream" at bay all through the day.

The night brought back the dream. I wondered if it was a dream. The structure came nearer, and I could see more details. It was rectangular and dark coloured, perhaps dark grey, there appeared to be no windows or even a door. The roof was domed, and it was shiny and gleamed in the starlight. I kept on towards it, and when I was about ten feet away, I could see that the structure had a rounded depression in the wall in front of me. I went towards it and stood before it. I wanted to knock but was hesitant because I did not know what to expect. I tried to listen to sounds from within, but there was no sound. I knocked on the depression softly, but my knocking made no sound. I now banged hard and still there was no sound. I waited to see if anything would happen. After a long time of waiting, I decided to push the depression and when I did a circular opening appeared. It was big enough for me to enter, so I entered. I was in a chamber which seemed huge and if it had walls they were too far to be visible. There was faint illumination, and I could not see anything there, so I kept moving forward. I was too frightened to make any sound and I kept shuffling forward.

The bell jolted me awake, and I woke up feeling relieved. All through the day, I managed to stay focused and waited for night to see what would happen. In the evening, I realised that I just did not think about the mystery of the girls all day.

Night brought sleep, and I was back in the chamber moving forward slowly but seemed to be getting nowhere. When I turned around, I still could not see anything. It was like being in a void. I clapped my hand, and there was no sound. I shouted as loud as I could, but I could not even hear myself. Soon I got fed up with nothing happening, so I just sat down to wait. I decided to meditate. After a long time, I opened my eyes to see that there was a golden yellow light permeating through the room. This light became bright, so bright that I could barely keep my eyes open. Suddenly there was a flash that I blinked. When I opened my eyes, I saw a person standing in front of me. It was hard to make out if it was a man or a woman. The person wore a golden robe and was much taller than me.

I had to crane up to see the face. When I saw the face, I was enchanted by the peace that radiated from it. Any fears that I had melted away. I wanted, to say something but could not open my mouth.

I was disappointed when the bell woke me up, and I reluctantly went to the practice of the day. I wanted just to go to sleep so that I could be back in the dream. Somehow I completed the exercises for the day and went to bed.

I was back in front of the person from last night. The person kept gazing at me, and I wondered if I should say something. The peace radiating from this person kept me silent. I did not want to break the spell. I just stood rooted to the spot and waited. The person finally signed to me to sit, and both of us sat down.

As I sat there, the person extended a hand and so did I because I felt that I should. When the person touched my hand, I felt that connection because I could now "hear" this person even though its lips did not move. "My name is Om", said the being. "We have given you many sleepless nights, Anil," said Om. "There is a lot to tell you, and we did not know how to do it without alarming you further," I looked at him/her with amazement. I wondered how he knew my name. "We communicate telepathically and can read your mind," said Om. "We have no gender, so it is alright to call me he or she," said Om, clearing my confusion.

"Who are you? And where am I" I said. "You are still sleeping, and we are communicating with you through your dreams," said Om.

The bell rang, and I had to wake up

CHAPTER 4

The Guardians

I had just two more days at the camp, and I wanted to make the most of them. I was not sure if I could carry on communicating with Om after leaving the retreat.

Night came and with it sleep. I was again in front of the being called Om waiting for more.

I found myself sitting in front of him again. He spoke "I know you have a lot of questions, and I also know what they are." "We have been trying to communicate with you, but it was not possible because usually your mind-chatter is too loud for us to get through." "We are the guardians, and I am the manifestation of them" "Our job is to preserve order and regulate nature on this planet" "I will explain more about us as I go along but first let me say that we will not harm you or anyone else. We are here to help." "In this situation that you are facing, you need all the help we can give". "Humanity may be under a grave threat and the problem that you are investigating is connected with that."

Every night while I was at the camp Om communicated with me and explained the situation and gave me a method to regularly communicate with him only while I slept.

The guardians were spiritual beings evolved from spiritual masters who had left the body and existed in the spirit dimension. Their job was to keep the planetary vibrations high and protect mother earth from harm. They had had a difficult time protecting mankind from itself, but now the threat was from outside, which was worse.

The world had faced many threats in the past, and the Guardians had taken care of them most of the time without the need for human intervention. This time, the threat involved persons who were working with beings from another planet and some human intervention was required. Catastrophic events had happened before and every time that this had happened, it had resulted in destruction. If the guardians failed, this time, another catastrophe would ensue, the whole planet enslaved by extra-terrestrials.

What I learnt chilled me to the bone. It was so hard to believe that I was sure that it would be a difficult fight. I would have to do it on my own because no one in the department or outside was going to believe me. Om was going to try and communicate with other people who could receive his communication and create support. How long that would take and how many would help was an unknown at this point. My job was to get the human enemy out of the way. But these people were strong and powerful and greedy and were being easily manipulated to help these aliens. We did not even know for sure who these people were. Om was only certain about one of them.

The aliens had made contact with humanity. Unfortunately, they had made contact with the wrong people. Perhaps it suited them because they had plans which were certainly not good for the population of Earth. The people they were in contact with were using the knowledge from the aliens to get richer and more powerful. They did not realise that they were becoming pawns of the aliens. Man's greed was leading to his downfall, and I was not going to let it happen. For once life had presented me with an opportunity to really make a difference, and I was not going to allow my fears to hold me back. My restlessness increased but this time, I welcomed it.

On my way back from the Vipassana camp I was excited and upset but not peaceful as I normally was after the ten-day retreat. I was ready for what I had to do but needed answers to a lot of questions. Even Om and the other Masters did not know all the facts, so a lot depended on me, and I did not have a clue about what to do next.

I wondered why the girls were being picked up; we knew it was the aliens behind this and did not know why. Why only girls from India? Was this fact correct? Was this happening in other countries too and their governments were not willing to reveal it?

I wondered how many more girls had been taken, and this got clear when I joined office on Monday. The number of girls had now risen to 27, and again it was random, and the age range was the same. I thought it may be a good idea to get them screened for electronic implants, but my seniors were not willing to sanction this. I made calls to the ones whom I had met earlier, and they did not report any unusual occurrence. The only thing that they said was that they were feeling very energetic and positive and doing much more work than before. They were sleeping much better than before. No one had approached them by anyone that they did not know before. They had not received any communication from anyone. I asked them to report anything unusual to me.

On Monday night, I decided to go to bed as soon I had my dinner. Once again I soon found myself sitting in front of Om. Before I could ask, he told me that I had doubts about him being one of the aliens, and he wanted to remove my doubts. He asked me if I would be willing to accompany him and meet the other guides. Once again he pre-empted my question by telling me that I would have to listen to my heart after meeting all the guides and make up my mind about trusting them.

Everything seemed possible in this dream-world. Om took my hand, and we started floating away. Almost instantly we found our self in a bowl surrounded by high mountains. The moonlight here was high and I could see that we were standing in front of what looked like a temple. It reminded me of the Madurai Meenakshi temple that I had visited long ago. This temple, however, was not in the middle of a city, but it was in the midst of a thick forest by the side of a fast-flowing river. We entered through big doors made of wood that had myriads of carvings of familiar Hindu Gods.

Inside there was a massive pillar less hall with a ceiling so high that I could not see it. The light was bright but did not hurt the eye. I could not see the source of illumination. I looked at the centre of the hall where I could see a circle of people dressed just like Om. There was an aura of peace around them. I was overwhelmed by a feeling of love. I do not have any other words to describe the feeling that I was experiencing. All of them turned to look at me as I approached. Some of them were fair skinned, and some were dark complexioned. They looked middle aged, and they radiated strength.

One of them rose and embraced me when I reached them. "I am Shanti, welcome"; he said and beckoned me to join the circle. I was too awed to say anything. I realised that I did not see his lips move. He must have noticed the look of surprise on my face and he said "we do not need language or sound to communicate. We can communicate directly with your mind. You have been brought here so that you can experience us and ask what you need to remove any doubts". Suddenly all my doubts and fears were all put to rest. I knew that these beings were beings of pure love and would not do any harmful act.

In an instant, I got that here was a group of evolved beings. These were Souls that had evolved to higher realms. These Souls had inhabited human bodies and even bodies on other planets far away. Their sole purpose was to preserve the balance of nature and foster an environment for real evolution to take place, evolution to a point where a soul need not be born again, a soul free from the cycle of birth and death. Sentient beings on many planets had the reached a point that they did not need a body any longer. Here on earth even though civilization had "developed", it was more a physical development rather than a real evolution of the spirit. The result was that man's capacity for self-destruction was growing faster than his spiritual development. The masters had to work hard to stop mankind from destroying itself. They had almost failed a few times when mankind brought itself to the point of extinction. They had managed to save them.

Now once again mankind was destroying this self-sustaining planet and to add to this mess an aggressive invader from another planet had sent scouts to earth. The Scouts' purpose was to pave the way for the invaders. The scouts were few and were like shapeshifters, hard to detect. The guardians knew that they were here on the planet and needed support to identify and defeat them on the physical plane. The big challenge for the Guardians was some influential people who were being manipulated by the aliens, and they had no clue about this. Their greed and hunger for power made them blind.

I took leave of the masters and soon woke up. It was a beautiful day, and I felt a sense of purpose and determined that I must do something. I still did not have answers to my questions and did not know where to start. My day at the office did not begin very well because my boss informed me that they had decided to close the investigation into the "temporary" abductions calling them an elaborate hoax perpetrated by unknown persons. I decided to keep shut and pursue this later. However, I decided to speak to a journalist friend and asked her to write a story about these girls. I did not share my information about the alien invasion because there was no way that anyone would believe the story about my dreams. I was hoping that the story would stir something up, and that may give me a few leads.

The next day brought news of two more girls who had experienced the "temporary" abductions and my boss again assigned me to interview the girls. There was nothing different about their experience. I was able to use this to convince my boss to keep me in the case and also to make a statement to my reporter friend that we had managed to get clues and were on the verge of a breakthrough in this case. We also took permission from the girls for their pictures to be used in the article with the hope that someone may have seen something.

The article appeared in the Sunday edition of a leading English newspaper. This story was picked up by the television stations. My interview was broadcast by one of the stations. Lots of public attention was attracted.

The article and the coverage by the television stations did not produce the result we wanted.

CHAPTER 5

The Scouts

Markov, the scout, looked at his companion. They were both feeling very uncomfortable wearing the breathing device. The atmosphere on this planet was unbreathable, and a lot of eco-engineering would be required for it to be inhabitable. We chose to land on earth because of the abundance of tomu, water or paani as spoken by earth people and a lot of the green stuff (hara) that grew in abundance here.

The telepathic abilities made it possible to communicate with these strange people and it was taking time to understand them and their weaknesses. The ones identified so far were easy to influence and would make it easy to take over this planet. Most of these people were greedy and hence easy to manipulate. The majority chose not to think for themselves and had a blind belief in "GODS". There were so many of these Gods that these people believed in, asking them for protection and forgiveness, expecting them to perform "miracles".

Inquiry soon revealed that many people were exploiting this blind belief in the power, and something called "money" that they used as an exchange for goods and services. Money was used to exploit and enslave people without their even knowing it. The element OGC (gold as it was called here) had absurd value considering that it was used mostly for ornaments. The precious stuff grew in abundance, and these earth people had no regard for it. It was good that this planet supported the growth of all these green growths. The plan was to use this world for growing this green stuff with earth slaves. This planet also had enough resources for them to manufacture their atmosphere here. They would have to live in domed cities.

It had taken two earth years to study to decide strategy and the sites most suitable for the initial landings to take place. The best place identified was one of the nations which were most vulnerable. The majority of the earthlings here had a slavish mentality, blind faith in "Gods" and greed for "money" They were also easily influenced by the female sex. These three could be used to influence and control these people easily.

The Scouts had the job of creating a situation where their populations would be allowed to land peacefully on this planet. The aggressive method rejected because it was costly and time-consuming.

They found out that on this planet, just like their own, there were the influencers. They had identified the right person to work with. The subject which they had contacted was a big "leader" of these people and quite influential. He was the "home minister" of this "country". He was the shortest physical specimen of this species that they had seen but brilliant being. He also had the gift for influencing people. The plan was to help him become powerful enough to be able to be of great help to them and facilitate landings on earth without any resistance.

They had offered him ten bars of OGC to show him that they were helpful people. They had also showed him some simple tools from their planet, which, for him were surprising and useful. He wanted the know-how to manufacture them. These gifts made him believe that the aliens would support him to get to a top position in his country. He pledged to help them.

At this time, he had no idea what they wanted. The scouts were looking to have one million such people in one earth year. They carefully selected females and teleported them to their scout ship, fitted them with the bio-implants and sent them back. These controlled women would influence others to be compliant. The small challenge faced was that they could not be sent back to the places where they been picked them up and part of their ships atmosphere congealed on them during the teleportation back to earth. These bio-implants that they harboured would be activated when the time was right, and these females would do the tasks of influencing groups that they would infiltrate. The bio-implants needed time to incubate before they became active.

They had two earth years for complete preparations here before the fleet could reach close enough for landing parties. Markov and Krock were the only scouts here.

They missed their planet with its green atmosphere and hoped that when the landing happened here, and they would be able to prepare this world in the time before their home planet ceased to exist. Their vast population needed resettlement in case they were not able to save it.

They wished they had an unlimited supply of bio-implants so that the process could be faster. Their supply of the essential green stuff was not going to last very long. Even if they wanted to use a more aggressive option, it would be difficult to take on these humans. At this time, they had only six small space ships, not enough for an aggressive invasion.

But the plan was going well, and they would succeed in landing the ships with the help of the humans who would be in their control. So far it seemed that the landing would happen peacefully.

CHAPTER 6

It Escalates

The next day in the office we received reports about twelve more TAs (temporary abductions) and this time, the profile of the girls was different. Even though they were of the same age group, these girls were from rural areas and had education up to high school.

I was wracking my brains to find out the reason these particular girls were selected. The only common attribute seemed to be that they were exquisite looking and articulate. I was sure that these abductions had something to do with the aliens but had no way to confirm this or to find anything out anything out of the ordinary about these girls after the abductions.

I continued our campaign to keep media focus on the TA's. So far nothing had turned up. I decided to keep contacting these girls and talk to them to find out what they were up to. I went to Delhi and contacted Mansi again.

She was friendly, and we decided to meet for dinner. It was nice to interact with her, and I found so many things we had in common. I was a lonely bachelor, and my job had never given me many chances for socializing. I had no friends or acquaintances of the opposite sex. This evening with Mansi was unusual for me. She spoke, and I listened, the only time I spoke was to ask a few questions about her routine before and after her TA episode. I was beginning to feel an attraction to her that I had never felt for anyone else. I was happy that we had the same educational background and interests. Her father was a business person and their family had lived in different cities during her childhood.

My life with my strict father was difficult. He had always made me feel small and insignificant and ridiculed me for not doing well academically. I finally escaped when I went the college. Hostel life forced me to develop some confidence. My desire to prove myself lead me to join the IPS where my determination to prove my father wrong made me work very hard and I made a name for myself. I was chosen for the challenging assignments and so far had managed to solve baffling crimes.

This case, however, seemed to be far more complicated than I could imagine. I was an atheist, a disbeliever in anything esoteric. I was so happy that I had agreed to do Vipassana meditation. This scientific method appealed to me, and I had done it many times. Had it not been for this I may never have been picked by the guides to help them. I was not sure how they knew about Suresh Kumar, the leader who was the aliens contact. I trusted what they said and resolved to investigate him.

The first thing I did was to find an opportunity to infiltrate his home and office. I needed someone inside. An opportunity arose when we discovered that a servant was required in Sureshs' house. We sent one of our operatives to take up the job. We could not put someone in his office, so we bribed his peon to become our informer. To do this was a little risky but we felt that his greed and fear would make him toe the line. We also stationed some people as sweepers around the house. I was hoping to get sanction for wiretapping and video surveillance but was not able to justify this to my superiors.

We got a lucky break when two of the TAs turned out to be from Suresh's constituency. Suresh was pressurising our department to do something, so I was sent to meet him. I quickly got an appointment and went to meet him. He turned out to be an imposing personality but spoke Hindi in a very rural accent. He dressed typically in a white dhoti and kurta. I gave him a details of actions taken in this case and then asked him if he had had any strange visitors in the last few months. This question upset him, and he terminated the meeting immediately. I wondered why he was angry. I was now hoping that our operative in his house may give me a lead about what was happening there.

I wanted to have all the girls watched but did not have the resources available. However, I managed to get two operatives attached to two of the girls, and I was in touch with Mansi so I would watch her myself. Nothing happened for three months, and my bosses were again getting restless and wanted me to handle other cases too. I took on another case and soon resolved it. By the third month, I got reports from our two operatives that both girls had become active socially. One had joined the chapter of one of the politically backed social organisation; the other had started a religious group and was acquiring a large following. People had begun calling her Gauri Amma. In the meantime, Mansi had become philosophical and had begun giving talks to ladies groups and was even getting invited to Rotary meetings and other such events.

I started inquiring into the other girls, and I found that every one of them had become active socially. They had either joined politics or other social groups. Four of them had become religious leaders of some sort. This was too much of a coincidence for me. It all looked very innocent except for the fact that all of them were TA's (temporary abductees). There was nothing I could do because none of them was doing anything objectionable.

I sometimes wondered why I got involved in this and why did I believe in a dream. I was in the fray, and it would help if I got some reassurance. Something to tell me, that I was not wasting my time. Even the girls who had been through the TA experience seemed better off and were doing well. Why was I reading something sinister in what these girls were experiencing? Mansi seemed so happy about her speaking engagements. She said that she was a shy person, who would who avoid meeting strangers and would never speak in front of a group. She was thrilled about what she was doing.

It was two years since the first abduction and all the reports about the girls did not suggest that they were doing anything harmful or illegal. They seemed to be doing social work that was helping people and was very popular with everyone they came in contact.

These girls were doing something to attract so many followers. Typical social workers did not have such a large following.

CHAPTER 7

The Movement

My meetings with Mansi became regular. We were meeting as often as my work would allow me. I found that I was getting on with her better than I had with anyone else, man or woman. I had no romantic inclinations but having her as a friend made me feel good. She started confiding in me and shared all her accomplishments with little girl enthusiasm. She had got a promotion at her firm and headed the PR division.

She was making a lot of friends and started having regular parties at her house. Guests were intellectuals who would engage in intense conversations about politics and the state of the country. The group that she interacted with felt very strongly about our nation not getting the prominence in world affairs despite being an exporter of so much intellectual manpower. They seemed disturbed by the increasing poverty and crime. They blamed TV for fanning the flames of dissent.

I was happy for Mansi and glad that she was becoming such an influence. She got very friendly with five other girls of her age; they did everything together. We started calling them the six sisters. Five of these girls started study circles for poor teenagers, and these study circles had more than 100 children each. They were helped to polish their language and math and were encouraged to enrol more children to join these study circles.

I now initiated inquiries into the other girls and found that all of them, without exception, had either started a social organisation, a study circle, religious group or a political organisation. None of these girls had shown any interest in social work before their abductions. Now they were in leadership roles where a large number of people held them in high esteem. One interesting fact that came to light was that each one of them mentored five girls, just as Mansi had done. These girls had also set up study circles. Those in rural areas were making groups where teenagers were taught skills to help them earn a livelihood, in addition to primary education. All these children were being encouraged to take an interest in earning money through agriculture too. They were specially invited to grow particular kinds of plants. The work that these girls were doing was excellent.

No adverse reports were coming in about TAs, so officially inquiry into this phenomenon was stopped. I was curious about their activities because it was incredible that they could get out of a traumatic experience like this and do so well. I decided to keep investigating Suresh Kumar because I was curious about his reaction to my innocent query. The newspapers reported that he was becoming very strong politically, and his son had started an industry that was manufacturing solar cells reported at prices much below what was there in the market. No one had any inkling of this new technology that was being used by him. It was apparent that alien technology was being used.

I had not dreamt about Om ever since I came back from Vipassana and wondered if that experience was a figment of my imagination. One weekend I did not have any plans to go out, so I sat down to meditate. When I was in deep meditation, I was once again transported to the big "temple" to meet with the Guardians. I again felt the same peace in their presence. What they shared with me was disquieting. They shared that what they were able to pick up telepathically from the aliens indicated that their plans were going well, and they somehow were more confident. Something was going to be "activated" soon. It was vital to find out what it was. One thing was clear, and that was that the aliens had no intentions of peaceful co-existence. They were clearly going to enslave the planet after the initial period of settling in.

What they shared about Suresh was even more disquieting. He was becoming very dominant in his party, and a majority of people were keen to make him the prime minister. Suresh Kumar was patronising many small and large companies and promised them cutting edge technologies for profit. His slogan now was that India would lead the world in technology.. He claimed that for the first time in history, we would eradicate poverty. India would become the richest country in the world. The guardians were picking up thoughts about his links with the aliens who were helping with the technology and also with gifts of Gold bars. The only good news from the Guardians was that they had contacted more people like me whom they could communicate with, and they would put them in touch with me.

Suresh Kumar was a man of humble beginnings; his father was a shopkeeper in a village. Suresh had managed an education and had graduated in science. He had been jobless for a while and then joined a political party. He worked hard and impressed everyone with his zeal. He was rewarded with a ticket for the election and won. His rise in the party had been fast, and he had become the Home Minister by time the alien scouts approached him.

The newspapers and media were giving Suresh a lot of attention. There was a lot of curiosity about his sudden rise to power and all this talk about technology from a rustic person like him. Soon this conversation died down, and some said that all those who raised such questions were threatened to stop. Suresh was the new messiah. He was genuinely working for the betterment of the country. People in his party were awed by this sudden change in the man and his way of working. Even the opposition party respected him. All this, for me, was proof of what the guardians said.

Two days after my nocturnal visit to the guardians, I got twelve phone calls. These were from people who had been asked to contact me. We decided to meet the same evening. One of them owned a company, and we met in a conference in his office. It was an interesting group of thirteen people. I introduced myself, Anil Khatri, IPS. Our host was a tall, fair Kashmiri gentleman, Mr. Arun Pandit, who ran a business manufacturing pens. One of the ladies present was a well-known political correspondent Ms. Kavita Khaitan. She was bold and known for her fearlessness. The other lady was a well know author and activist, Renu Sharma. There was Mr. Kishore Talwar, Chief of the Intelligence Bureau, a tall person with piercing eyes. Mr. Karan Kumar was a young business person who ran a printing press. Mr. Ahmad Hussain, a very elderly person with a grey beard, he had an export business. A man from Tamil Nadu who called himself "Srini" short form for Srinivasan, he was a folk singer and musician. There was Professor Krishan Sahu, from Bihar. The only Sardarji in the room was Gurjeet Singh, who had a manufacturing business in Ludhiana. Mr. Alfred Roberero was a pugnacious young person who was from Mumbai, and he ran a modelling agency. A small statured man of indeterminate age introduced himself as Gautam Bose, he was from Delhi and was a realtor. A very dark and tall person introduced himself as Mr Arpit Johri, who had a car distributorship. This diverse group had one thing in common, they were all practitioners of Vipassana Meditation, and every one of them had 'met' the guardians. This fact automatically caused us to trust each other. Typically the presence of a police officer and an IB chief would have caused some uneasiness.

After the introductions, there was silence for a while. Kavita started the conversation. "What are we supposed to do?" There was silence, and all of them looked at Mr. Talwar. "I am as much in the dark as you are and can do nothing officially, he is likely to be the next PM," he said. Everyone felt that the best thing to do would be to wait and be alert to developments. Kavita and Kishore also had access to information that they would pass on to us.

We would keep in touch and meet when required. At the end of the meeting Mr. Kishore Talwar and I walked out together and stood outside talking. Mr. Talwar had a lot of information about the TA girls and was curious about my findings. I shared my intention to keep an eye on them and their activities, and he was also willing to deploy some of his people to maintain an eye on them. Both of us were clear that there was something going on, and we had to do something to forestall any sinister plans of the aliens and their collaborators like Suresh Kumar. It was reasonable to suppose that if Mr. Suresh Kumar was roped in by the scouts, then there must be others and we had to find them.

I decided to would allot more manpower to this task and requested this entire "group of thirteen" to inform me if they noticed anything unusual. I also gave them the names of the girls who had been abducted (TA's) and asked them to be open to any news about them in their cities.

While driving back, I got a call from one my operatives who were keeping an eye on Suresh Kumars' residence. For the first time, we had a concrete lead, and it added to my worry.

CHAPTER 8

Developments

My operative from the ministers' house reported that there had been, at least, three visits by two strange looking persons to the ministers' home. While all regular visitors were made to wait before being taken in to meet the minister, these two were ushered in immediately and they spent more time than usual, sometimes even one full hour. Tea and biscuits were usually served to visitors who stayed for so long, but in this case, nobody was allowed inside to serve anything. Our operative had placed a listening device that was able to record only what the minister said. It seemed that the other parties had always remained silent.

I listened to the first recording which went like this. Minister "Thank you for what you are doing. We have stated the manufacture, and the product is good" ...... silence............... Minister "whatever more you can give will help a lot. "Silence .... Minister "you will ensure that? How can I be sure? I believe what you say, but we must make sure that we will not be harmed." …….. silence……………………………….. for almost half an hour and then "this is amazing, may I visit it? Oh, I can arrange that ".

The recordings of the next two visits of these strange people were completely blank except for the sound of water being poured into a glass or the creaking of a chair and some footsteps.

The operative had gave me three photographs of the strange visitors and told me that these people never spoke to anyone. They had strange eyes, yellowish green colour, unlike any that he had seen before. These men were around six feet tall, and they had mongoloid features. Their skin was leathery. They had a funny gait. Very jerky and when they walked there was a weird squishy sound like when people stepped in a puddle.

The operative who was placed outside the house had followed them each time, but they could evade him easily by literally disappearing. He also confirmed their strange gait and the sound they made when they walked. What my men found very odd was that these people were just twenty meters in front of them and in none moment they just vanished.

The operatives kept their vigil, and this was rewarding. Three days after the last visit, they came again at dusk. The minister quickly came out got into his car with them and drove off. The car had gone for about half a kilometre when it came to a lonely stretch of road, where it disappeared. He returned late at night and looked pale and shaken up. The next day he kept to his bedroom and did not even ask for a cup of tea.

The next couple of weeks were hectic at the Suresh Kumar household. There were many visitors, mostly party officials and leaders. Suresh Kumar's' wife came from the village. There was something brewing and then everyone got the news that Suresh was the new PM. People were euphoric to hear this news, and there were noisy celebrations with fireworks.

It was surprising how well everyone took the announcement. The industrialists welcomed it. The media hailed it. The farming community was rejoicing saying that their saviour had come. Even the opposition had kind words to say about him. It seemed like his strategy to become PM had worked very well. Our group of thirteen was sure that the aliens had a role to play.

On a Saturday evening, I met Mansi to find her beaming. When I asked, she said that she was euphoric that Suresh Kumar had become the PM. She went on and on about his virtues and how good he was for the nation. I was shocked to learn that her group of intellectuals were all in agreement with her. I was on the verge of telling her but held back because the thirteen had agreed that we would not tell anyone without the concurrence of all the others. The six sisters as I called them and all their groups had the same opinion. I wondered what would happen if they found out the truth about Suresh. It was three years since Mansi had been abducted.

I quickly called Kishore and asked him to find quickly about all the TAs and the groups they represented. Within a day, he came back with the information that all the girls and the groups they represented were unanimous in their support of the new PM.

The circle of influence of the 29 girls had extended to more than 100000 people and was growing fast. Each was influencing two more people and so on. It was like a tidal wave of popularity and by the time the PM assumed office we were sure the number would triple. There were staunch supporters of his in almost every walk of life.

The new PM took office and within a week, and announced grand plans for the development of the country. I was listening to his speech and liked what I was hearing. He touched upon almost every area of concern of the ordinary man. What I liked the most was that he vowed to stop communal clashes and took steps to ensure that these conflicts did not happen. He also got rid of unnecessary red tape that was a big impediment for anyone who wanted to start a new business enterprise. I was sceptical because all politicians made many promises and I wondered how many promises he would keep.

He announced the formation of 6 unique zones with a lot of fanfare and said that there would be huge employment opportunities in each one of them. All these zones were away from populated areas but near the sea and not very far from forests. Now development would reach these remote locations. These areas were cordoned off, and security forces were deployed all around them. The areas cordoned off were huge; a small sized city could be accommodated in each. These areas were enclosed by 20 foot high thick walls. Once the walls were erected, no one was allowed inside.

After the initial announcement, there was no mention of what was being done in these zones. Complete secrecy was maintained. Those who asked were told that these zones were the place from where a New and Prosperous India would emerge.

The TAs in the meantime had created a huge group of volunteers, all women whose job was to fan out to the villages and "help" village people. All these groups were being funded by unknown sources and no one from the media had come forward so far to do an expose. After all, this was a good cause. All religious organisations, Hindu, Muslim, Jain, Christian, Sikh and others encouraged their youth to participate in this nation-building task. We were witnessing a historical event, all religious groups working together.

A huge workforce was also created from rural areas by these volunteers. These were soon employed around the six special zones. There they were engaged in building living areas all around the walls of the particular areas. The enthusiasm levels were high; the pay was good, so work progressed fast. Soon each special zone was surrounded by enough dwellings to accommodate 20000 workers, supervisors and managers. Each of the six satellite cities had two schools and two hospitals and entertainment and shopping areas.

There was a special security force formed to guard these special zones. These were better equipped than the police and were issued automatic weapons. The commanders were deputed from the military. The security forces had their accommodation. These formed the inner cordon, and the worker dwellings were in the outer cordon. The big two walls had two massive gates. By the time all these buildings had come up, other infrastructure like roads had been built. There was a helipad outside each special zone. Power lines to all these were laid from the special zones to the outside dwelling units. Power from inside would come only when the special zones became operational. Temporary power was provided by generators to the homes already occupied.

We the thirteen were aware of the special zones and what was happening around them and were not sure if we should celebrate this achievement of the nation or to be fearful. It looked like the great walls would enclose huge industrial units that would benefit everyone.

Our new PM initiated a development program where all parties were fully involved and for the first time, there was unity of purpose. The opposition was supporting affirmative action and not making things difficult for the government. For the first time since our independence, there was one purpose and that was – "India will be number 1".

Never before had I seen such a propaganda blitz urging people to work hard. The public was being called to work for the country, and there were "India number 1" posters everywhere. In rallies, in school assemblies, wherever people assembled there was one slogan shouted that was "India number 1". The people became proud to be Indian. The country and its population were being enrolled into a vision.

Our group of thirteen was happy with what was happening. What was going on so far was good and many of the good things were those that we had dreamed of. Our guardians were still warning us to be careful and not forget that the aliens were influencing our PM, and they could misuse this authority.

There was nothing we could do except to wait and see what happens. A time for action would come.

CHAPTER 9

The Landings

It was a year since the PM had announced the special zones. The construction of the special zones was complete and an inauguration ceremony announced on 13 January. It was fifteen days from the date of the announcement.

The PM asked for a meeting with his cabinet. Here he made a statement that paved the way for the creation of a new world history. All of the cabinet members were first sworn to secrecy, and then Suresh Kumar informed them about how he had been secretly approached by representatives of a very advanced alien race. This race wanted to start a relationship with planet earth and had chosen India as their trade partner. Their study of the world had found India and its people most suitable for this partnership. He said that India was fortunate that it would have access to technology that no one on the planet possessed, and this would make us the most prosperous nation on Earth. All that these aliens wanted from India was six places where they could establish trading and technology outposts. Also, they wanted to grow grasses and fast growing trees that they would process and send back to their planet.

The aliens insisted that they would not like any contact with anyone except India, and they wanted assurance about this. They would, in turn, give us protection and support on defence matters. They would keep to themselves and not venture out of their locations. All contact would only be through their scout-ambassadors. Each member got a small gift; it was a bar of Gold. There was no doubt that the deal with the aliens would benefit India and all the members all agreed with the plan. The parliament approved the plan.

The PM made the announcement to the people of our country. I was impressed by his oratory. He told the people that God had sent people from the stars to help us get back into the golden age as we had been centuries ago. The people loved it and looked forward to a great future. A few people questioned the deal and wondered if there could be a threat from the aliens. No one listened to them.

The Scouts were given permission, and they passed on the message to their fleet. The fleet would arrive in a month. Elaborate preparations were being made to meet and greet them. TAs who had spread to significant numbers allayed any fears that people had and people started looking forward to the visit of those "celestial" beings. The superstitious, God fearing people of India quickly accepted that these were "Gods "from the skies and fear turned to expectation.

The foreign powers that got the news started pestering the PM to be allowed to meet the aliens, but all their efforts were in vain. The pressure was brought to bear, and there was no effect. They were politely informed that if they cooperated, they would get to get some share of the trade. Pressure eased off, and the foreign players started trying clandestine means to find out more about the aliens. The Americans stepped up their security and so did the Europeans, they were afraid that the aliens may have hostile intentions, and they wanted to protect themselves.

The day of the arrival dawned. The media from all over the world turned up and were allowed into the special press zone. The general public was accommodated in special viewing platforms along with the media well outside the walls. There were also a lot of tourists who came specially to see the landings, and they had to buy special permits. There was a special viewing gallery set up to accommodate them. When the time came, we saw the sky darken, and people eagerly looked at the heavens and saw them. Six pyramid shaped objects that grew bigger and bigger. One came down, and the others headed for their designated special zones.

Kishore and I had managed to become a part of the official welcoming committee at site number one that was in Orrisa. We and the PM and his entourage watched the pyramid getting larger. It came down silently, and we were surprised about that because we expected some sound. There was a lot of static electricity in the air, and I felt a tingling all over my skin. As the "Pyramid" got closer, it started looking huge and looked exactly like the pictures of pyramids I had seen. The surface was not smooth and was a shiny muddy brown in colour. It settled in the middle of the circular zone. We were apprehensive and hoped that nothing bad would happen. I hoped there would not be any unpleasant surprises.

After a long wait, there was a flash of light. It was a door opening on one side of the craft. The scouts who had come with our delegation went up to meet their brethren. A ramp emerged from the triangular door, and a tall being came down. A huge being stepped out; he looked like a human, but the face was different. It was flatter and had a greenish cast. The scouts kneeled down to welcome their leader. He "spoke" something to the scouts who stood up and turned to face the humans.

All three of them walked up to the welcoming committee. The members had been briefed not to make any physical contact with the aliens. When they came close, all the delegates bowed. The leader of the aliens nodded back. The PM made a welcome speech that was watched by the whole world. The alien leader spoke inside the heads of all assembled at the site but the microphones picked up nothing. An anchor realised this and spoke out loud what he heard in his head. "We come in peace earth people; we come bearing gifts for your people. We wish to have trade with your people. We will give you gifts of technology and minerals that you need, and we want to cultivate, process and take the vegetable matter that we can use. We thank you for providing the structures for us to make our trading posts. We offer you a token our thanks."

As the leader said this, another door opened on the craft, and a large platform floated out towards the gathering. When it reached, one of the scouts lifted up the cloth covering it. There was a huge pile of gold there. One of the scouts said, "This is 10 tons and should more than cover your expenses for building the six trading outposts ". The leader then turned around and went back to the ship, leaving the scouts behind. The delegation had many questions and was disappointed because they did not get an opportunity to ask them. The scouts said,"

The Indian Resurrection

As we assured you before, we are the only ones whom you will see from now on, and we will answer all your questions. Our people will remain inside the ships. Atmosphere domes will be set up soon, and all our people will stay inside them."

We saw from news reports that there were similar landings in the other five zones but without any welcoming committees. The public and media were allowed to see the arrivals from outside the walls. My operatives who were stationed at all the landing sites reported that the Ships landed and after a short while a transparent dome enclosed it. The dome started just inside the circular wall that had been erected.

The group of thirteen watched all this with scepticism. One of them Srini, quipped that this was an East India Company from the stars. Our presence at the landing gave us nothing new, and there seemed to be nothing sinister. There had been nothing sinister when the East India Company started trading with India centuries ago. We were sure that it would not be good for us in the long run but with nothing concrete to offer we could not even muster support for opposing the designs of the aliens. We did not even know if their intentions were evil. It seemed like we had more to fear from other countries than these aliens at this time.

The aliens had erected glass-like domes inside the circular walls of all the domes. There were some kinds of force fields around them. This could be summarised by the fact that when birds touched it, they got fried. No one could see anything inside the domes because the domes were filled with a green coloured atmosphere. The domes had a method of communicating with each other and also with the scouts. The only contact with us humans was through the Scouts. They were the ambassadors of the aliens.

The aliens wanted us to grow special grasses outside the domes for them. The land had been earmarked for this near the domes outside the townships. The cultivation of the grasses was started on large tracts of land allocated for this purpose.

There was a conveyor belt built by the aliens. It came out of a hole in the wall, and it would be used to carry things in and out. It brought out knocked down parts of the desalination plants. These were to be assembled according to drawings that were provided. The government provided engineers and workers. They were housed in the township outside the walls. One such plant was built near the sea of each trading post. Desalinated water was piped to the fields where our workers planted the alien grass. This grass was quick growing grass that reached man height in two weeks. Our workers had to cut it and once cut it was sent through the conveyor into the dome.

A year had passed since the landings. Once a month a huge alien transport ship would arrive with 10 tons of gold and depart with the final product made inside the dome using the grasses we had grown for them. After three such deliveries of the gold, the PM told the Scouts that we needed something more valuable. Too much availability of gold had brought down the price.

We asked for technology that would allow us to make clean electricity. The aliens agreed and on the fourth trip, the supply craft brought parts for assembly of a power plant that needed no fossil fuels. It used sunlight and sand and rocks and produced electricity. The output was enough to power a small city. The first units were used to energize the satellite towns of the special zones.

Other units were used for powering up small cities and the power saved was diverted to rural areas that had not yet been receiving sufficient power. The benefits from the aliens were reaching the masses, and they were jubilant.

I was appointed to a committee that was asked to advise the PM about defence equipment that could be sourced from the aliens. The problem was that we did not know what they had, so we did not know what to ask. It was finally decided that we would ask the scout ambassadors to tell us about their weapons. If they were benign, they would have no problem telling us.

The technology to make the power units was not given to us, but the aliens were willing to give us 100 such units during each trip of the supply ship. India would soon be free from fossil fuels for power generation. Availability of more power had a positive impact on industrial output.

The aliens wanted more land for cultivating the grasses and special trees. Barren land near the outposts was allotted; water was piped in from the desalination plants. Soon these lands were giving abundant harvests and two supply ships were coming every month. Earth asked for more desalination plants and energy units. All this additional water and electricity also added to agricultural production in areas which had never grown anything. India was becoming more prosperous than ever before.

Our group of 13 met regularly, and all that we could discuss was how lucky we were to have these visitors from space with whom we had a symbiotic relationship. The Guardians, however, kept warning us. It was impossible for us to do anything against them in a country where everyone was getting so many benefits because of them.

We were also getting reports about the TAs and what we learnt astounded us. They now were running vast women organisations and these had millions of members. All of them were spreading the only positive news about the benefits of these celestial beings.

Five years quickly passed after the landings of the aliens. The ruling party won the elections quickly. No other government had brought so much prosperity to the people. The ruling party was good at leveraging the celestial connection and the TA's followers to achieve their ends. The TA's were fully committed to Suresh and his party. He was not only the PM but also the party supremo.

The foreign powers kept trying to make contact with the aliens, but the tight security around the domes made it impossible for them to do so. The aliens were just not willing to meet anyone. Since nothing very dramatic seemed to be happening, the interest on their side to meet the aliens started diminishing. They bitterly complained about the unfairness of the Indians in keeping such an important meeting to themselves. I suppose they were upset why India was the only trading partner of the aliens.

I was sent for a conference of Law enforcement agencies. The conference was in the New York and attended by officers from many countries. I was surprised that so many delegates wanted to talk to me. All of them had questions about the aliens and were surprised when I told them that no one had any contact with them. people were pestering me with questions about what we were getting from the aliens. I had been warned not to mention what we were getting. I had permission to share about what we were selling to these countries already, and I did.

One evening I was surprised to be approached by a beautiful woman who wanted to have a drink with me. I became suspicious when she showed interest in coming up to my room at the end of the evening. It seemed like I was walking into a honey trap so I politely declined the offer. The next day there was a more direct approach during lunch. An elderly gentleman who seemed to be an American approached me and said "we are interested in information about the aliens and are willing to pay for it "I decided to string him along and said, "what do you want to know?". He gave me a list, and when I looked at it, I realised how little I knew. I politely declined to tell him saying that it was impossible to get the information he wanted and why. He seemed surprised but left me alone after that.

When I returned to India, I informed my friend Kishore about this episode. He warned me to watch my back and get some protection from the department. The western powers would try their best to get to the aliens. Mansi was happy to see me back, and I was sure that my affection for her had helped me resist the honey trap.

One thing I understood from the conversation with the elderly man was that there was very little known about the aliens and that the foreign powers viewed them with suspicion and hostility. I had to prevent them from doing anything to harm the domes or the aliens. I alerted all my operatives around the domes. The foreign powers would try to hire people from our country, and they would not be so easy to detect. Our vigilance paid off when we were able to intercept an intruder who was trying to get in through the conveyer wearing breathing apparatus. His interrogation came to an end as soon as it started because he swallowed a cyanide pill.

We were sure that many such attempts would be made and waited for them to happen.

CHAPTER 10

Ambitions

The alien race was called the Zothar. After two years of trade, they asked the PM permission to establish two more special zones. These were to be twice the size of the old ones. These two also were to be very close to the sea with enough barren land for cultivation of the alien plants. They offered more of the desalination plants and power units. In addition, to this, our PM asked for platinum which he wished to trade for naval ships, submarines and jet fighters. His advisors felt that with these domes in coastal areas our defence would have to be enhanced.

The aliens informed us that they had installed intruder detection systems and laser-like defence systems. They also offered us the same to us to strengthen our national defences. With the promise of Platinum and the defence systems, the Zothar got permission to make two more domes. Like before townships were set up around the walled in area. These two new areas were huge, four times bigger than the initial outposts; it would take a year to complete our side of the work.

All this while I was assigned routine cases and that kept me busy. My friendship with Mansi continued. Her busy schedule now gave us fewer opportunities to meet. I was appointed as an Assistant Commissioner of Police. My mother was getting flooded by offers from parents of girls who found me quite eligible to marry their daughters. I kept fending off my mom but had no real reason for not marrying. My need for sex was taken care of by the occasional dalliance and I had not met anyone who appealed to enough for me to want to marry her. I thought a lot about Mansi and felt that she was the closest to being acceptable as a wife.

The new developments in the country were making us proud. I wondered if we were paranoid about the aliens but my trust in the Guardians made me keep an eye on the Scout-ambassadors. A few trusted team members and I had found nothing suspicious so far. Policing kept me busy and especially now because jealous neighbouring countries had stepped up terrorist activities and I had been specially assigned to take care of this. IB intelligence told us that our alliance with the aliens made our neighbours fearful, and fear makes people do crazy things. Our immediate neighbour had clerics who were whipping their followers into a frenzy saying that India had aligned itself with Shaitan, the devil himself.

Every few months we arrested jihadis based on intelligence inputs received. These were well-trained malcontents bent on causing trouble in our country.

Our defence forces were getting much stronger than before. We had doubled the number of our warships, submarines, jet fighters and tanks. We had increased the size of our army and given them weapons that they could only dream about before. We could now afford to buy the best body armour and helmets for our security forces and police. Our soldiers were equipped with the most advanced weapons. Our defence electronics were beyond compare. With the help of the aliens, we had detection systems that could detect any intrusion even from very low altitudes. We had laid deep underground cables for defence communications to maintain secrecy.

Our scientific minds that had emigrated started coming back because there were more opportunities for them in our country. We had the resources to invest in industries and our need to import was reduced. At the same time, air pollution was a real problem because of the number of vehicles being added to our roads. So the scientific minds were put to finding inexpensive non-fossil fuel using vehicles. A lot of money was being invested in this.

Better electric vehicles became the answer. With the technology provided by the aliens, we developed batteries that were cheaper and durable. Power was cheap and clean. With all this going on the aliens soon receded into the background. Only the government paid any attention to them.

I bought my first electric car, and it was light and fast. The best thing about it was that it was almost soundless. Mansi also bought one. In fact, most people had started selling off their fossil fuel vehicles. The demand for the gas guzzlers was going down.

All the car manufacturers had begun using the electric engines. They had no choice if they wanted to survive in India.

India was becoming a power and suddenly desired to use that power to make the world a better place. We decided that we would help eradicate the growing terrorism in the world. With this in mind, we started pressuring our neighbour to stop harbouring terrorists. When they expressed inability to do so, we decided to take matters into our hands and conducted strikes across the border and destroyed the terrorist training camps.

The world silently heaved a sigh of relief, and our neighbour threatened war. The world governments put pressure on them to be quiet. Their military that had never fully heeded their politicians decided to hit us where it would hurt us the most. They decided to strike at the alien outposts. They launched a clandestine seaborne assault. It failed because they could not get through. The attack was foiled by our special force defending the domes.

The scout - ambassadors, asked for details about these people. They were briefed about nuclear weapons and why this stopped us from attacking this neighbour. They suggested that we should make sure that the nuclear warheads and facilities in our neighbourhood should be neutralised. If we permitted, they would do it for us.

We allowed it, and I think it was a mistake because it was the first time they were coming out of their domes. The Zotharians demonstrated their might when there were mysterious explosions in Pakistan that destroyed their nuclear arsenal and production facilities. I was glad that the Zothar were our allies. We wanted to prevent China and North Korea from rearming the Pakistanis, and so we permitted the aliens to destroy their nuclear facilities and weapons. We denied them permission to do the same with other countries. The message was clear to all that India could not be trifled with.

This effectively neutralized any threat from that side of the border. Our other threat was China, and this sent a clear message to them too. The USA suspected the involvement of the aliens and raised this matter in the UN. We were able to dispel their fears, but their suspicions were aroused.

On my personal front life became easier because the terrorist problem was handled for now. I met Mansi twice in one week and found that she had affection for me. I proposed, and she agreed and said that she would ask her parents to speak to my mother and fix up the engagement, wedding, etc. This would be a new chapter in my life, and I was very excited. I was on top of the world.

Things in the country were getting better and better. We would soon have clean surplus power and perhaps be able to manufacture these power units. The Zothar did not agree to give us the technology but promised to give us as many units that we needed. So far in our trade with them, we seemed to be benefitting more than them, so we did not want to break our agreements with them. In any case any attempt to reverse engineer the power units only resulted in them melting. Melting like hot wax.

We got permission to sell the power units to other countries, and we had many buyers from many countries, but we gave preference to African countries and our neighbours. All surplus stocks were sold in a week, and the price of each would allow us to build a large school or a small hospital. We were also able to spare some desalination plants, and the Middle East grabbed them. This and many other things the aliens were giving us were making our country very rich. Another factor was that the flow of money to foreign fraudulent bank accounts stopped. Taxes in our country were the lowest in the world. This was also bringing in a lot of foreign investment.

Both the large domes were ready now and as soon as the grass production started the number of ships would increase to three a month. These domes were being used to relocate some of their citizens to Earth we found this out when they asked for land to grow their unique food. This migration to earth caused worry because we had a huge population of our own. Despite our problem, our government agreed.

Our group of thirteen saw this as the first sign of trouble to come, and we decided to do something. Kavita took on the job of getting the media to start making noise about it. Some stations talked about this but after the inaugural show, no more news about this appeared.

I happened to mention this to Mansi, and she was unperturbed saying that she knew about it. She stated that it was good that these celestial beings wanted to live here and were it not proving to be good for us so far? She was very convinced about this. I understood then how deeply many people believed in these aliens, and I wondered if we would ever be able to muster public opinion against these aliens. It may be too late by then.

The government announced the next general election and all of us in my department were busy with policing to ensure that all went well. The turnout at the elections was the highest ever and Suresh and his party once again got a clear majority.

Another two years had passed since the Zothar had landed. The Zothar food plants were grown, and a green powder had to be mixed in the soil for this. The plants grew into trees that bore large sized purple coloured fruit. The humans were warned that these would be poisonous to them, and this was proved when some stray dogs ate them and died on the spot. The aliens requested us to produce the green powder for them in facilities they built for us outside the domes. The raw materials were easily available except for one item that they supplied.

No one had any idea how many aliens were there in the six small domes and the two large ones. I wondered if anyone knew. We had to find a way and requested the Guardians if they could help. Since they could communicate telepathically just like the aliens, perhaps if may be possible to listen to the Scouts when they communicated with the PM. They said that they would make an attempt.

We the thirteen met to review the situation. On the plus side, we had a stable government thanks to the TAs and their supporters. This stable government had done a good job with the help of the Zotharians. Poverty was down, agriculture and farmers were doing well, the industry was doing extremely well and with the return of the brain power, many new technologies were developed and sold abroad. The platinum and gold that we got from the aliens were put to good use. Our defence forces were the strongest and best-equipped troops in the world. Our police force had equipment that even western police forces did not have. New bullet proof helmets, bulletproof vests and small two ways communication devices that functioned as closed secure wireless communicators for the police to talk to each other and the same handset could call or receive calls from any telephone. Our constables were all provided high-speed electric motorcycles.

On the negative side was the fear that one day we may be overrun and enslaved by the aliens, but there were no clear signs that they had such intentions.

One day the PM summoned the cabinet and announced that we should expand our territories to include Afghanistan, Pakistan, Bangladesh, Myanmar, Srilanka, Nepal and Tibet. Bhutan was already a protectorate. He justified it saying that they were a part of our nation before the British. Many in the government were afraid of the backlash from the western powers and China that the Prime Minister was confident that this could be dealt with. There was an agreement about this and with the knowledge about the strength of our armed forces parliament had no problem approving this plan. It was made clear to everyone that secrecy was paramount. If there were a leak from anyone, it would be dealt with sternly.

There were many like myself who wondered if it was prudent to risk all this progress for a war that could have disastrous consequences for the entire world. This view was shared by many people in the PMs Advisory group, but the PM assured them that public opinion in the western countries would not allow them to interfere in any conflict in this region. India was now known and recognised as rich and powerful, and a large number of their businesses were located here. It would not be in their interest to annoy India.

The plan was put to the Scout Ambassadors who, after consultations with their leaders came back to inform us that the Zothar had no objections and would help us if required. They advised us to wait for two years to make ourselves stronger and build up the military ordinance and personnel before taking action. They also requested permission to build another big dome near the sea in the Rann of Kutch.

Preparations to annex these countries began, and no one who was aware of this top secret plan was afraid of the consequences, if any, of what was being planned. We would wait till we were fully ready and also for the right opportunity to launch an attack.

Indians enjoyed technologies more advanced than many other countries. One example was our low-cost electric cars, and another was our mobile smartphones that had become so cheap that everyone had one. Internet speeds were extremely fast. The list was long.

What I liked the most was that our rural areas now had proper sanitation and water. Medical services there were so good that the villages came to the city only for major surgeries. Helicopter ambulances were freely available and subsidised so that they were affordable.

The world envied our progress and our nation revelled in its revival. This prosperity and growth also made many people very unhappy.

CHAPTER 11

The wedding

When we finally decided to marry, Mansi's parents were initially reluctant that their daughter wanted to marry a police officer. They wanted her to marry the son of an old friend who was also a prominent business owner. Mansi was resolute and persuaded them to meet me. This meeting convinced them that I was a suitable match for their daughter. We had our official engagement the week after. My mum insisted on this because she was scared that I may change my mind and wanted the wedding to happen soon. I was already forty years old and she did not want me to wait any longer. I was blissfully unaware of our governments' plan for war and I agreed to the wedding date.

My friends and my secret group were happy that I had decided to tie the knot. I discovered a lot of relatives who had been lying dormant for a long time. There were my late fathers' brother and his children who had not been in touch with for years. There were many of my relatives from my mother's side too. All this came up when my mother and I were planning a guest list. What a fuss! I left all these details of the wedding to my mother. If I had my way, we would have had a simple court marriage with a reception afterwards for a few friends.

The month passed quickly with planning the wedding and making all the arrangements typical to an Indian wedding. Mansi also agreed that we should avoid ostentation and have a simple wedding but we Mansi's parents did not agree as they wanted to celebrate the wedding of their only daughter with a big bang. They were a very wealthy business family and their family would expect this from them. I was happy that Mansi and I agreed on many things. We both did not want any children but we did not tell our parents for fear of disappointing them. Becoming grandparents were important to Indian parents.

The wedding celebrations lasted a week and soon and the reception was attended by more than 800 people. Only someone who has attended an Indian wedding will know about the number of ceremonies and how tiring it is for the bride and bridegroom. At the end of the celebrations, we were both exhausted but blissfully happy. It was also nice to know that I had so many good and loving people in my family.

After all the revelry, we flew away to Sikkim followed by Bhutan where we spent two idyllic weeks celebrating our new relationship. The beauty of these places is breathtaking and we enjoyed the mountains, the silence and the pristine air. We were so comfortable with each other that it felt like the dream. It was unbelievable that I could feel so close to anyone. It was almost like we could anticipate what the other wanted. So this is love I thought. I never realised that I was capable of so much tenderness; I thought my police job had made me incapable of soft feelings. I discovered the meaning of 'quality time.'

Our return brought us back to the routine of our jobs and I missed the time that we spent together. There was tension in the air in the government offices. The intentionality with which the officials went about their jobs was amazing. The sloth that pervaded these offices was missing now.

I heard disturbing news from the grapevine in the office that the country was preparing itself to wage war. Our country had never attacked another without provocation. I found this hard to believe especially because things were going so smoothly in our country and there seemed to be no external threat.

I spoke to some of my school mates who were in the army and they were very uncomfortable. One of them said that something was brewing because a lot of a high number of manoeuvres and drills. There was more secrecy than ever before.

At home, I found Mansi busy on the phone most of the time. There was something on her mind and she was tense. I had never seen her like this after the first time I had met her when she was shaken up. When I asked her, she told me that war was coming and she had a lot to do. I found it puzzling that she had such information but I kept mum.

In the next meeting of the thirteen, this came up. Our IB friend Kishore was aware of the preparations because he had been asked to gather military intelligence from all the neighbouring countries. Gathering such information was routine but never before were so many details asked. Other agencies whom he dealt with had also said the same thing. Almost all members of our small group always kept their ears to the ground and had heard similar rumours. I wondered if the aliens were behind this initiative.

Our first married year passed blissfully without any war happening and Mansi had returned to her usual self. We were a euphoric married couple. We often travelled to Dehra Dun to spend time with my mother; she loved her daughter in Law and they became good friends. Mansi would take over the cooking and made my mothers' favourite dishes. We would go for long peaceful walks together. I was happier than I had ever been. The only time we were apart was when I had to travel for an investigation or she had a speaking engagement outside the city. I had not told her about our secret group since she was as positive about the celestial beings as she called them. In fact, none of the married members had told their spouses.

Mansi once invited me to accompany her to one of the functions where she was speaking. I sat in the audience listening to her. She was a passionate speaker and she talked about the fact that we had a stable government that was able to achieve so much because of its stability. All this was also possible because it was getting the support of the celestials and using it for the benefit of the people. The guidance of the celestials and their material support hade made India a great nation like it used to be in olden days. We were becoming a model country and our influence would spread far and wide. The enthusiastic gathering gave a standing ovation at the end of the talk. After the talk Mansi was surrounded by people and all of them were singing the praises of our government and the celestial beings. I had a tough time dragging here away from her admirers.

I had heard such reports about the oratory of the other TA's too and I wondered if the aliens were somehow orchestrating this. Even if they were, it seemed to be achieving positive results so far. Our PM had become one of the most revered leaders since Gandhiji and there was no doubt that our country had progressed a lot since our contact with the aliens.

I wondered when we would erect temples in the name of the celestials. They were revered and never seen, just like Gods but unlike the Gods the aliens were helping us. I hoped that this symbiotic relationship would continue like this. The Guardians also wished for the same thing but were vigilant. So far they had not been able to read the Scout-ambassadors. One thing they had found out was that the life span of the average Zotharian was 200 earth years. The ones here were not the real leaders but were just doing the bidding of the real leaders on their home planet. According to their estimate, there were one million Zotharians in all the domed cities on earth.

Things were going very well for us in India and I was hoping our ambitions of waging war would get deferred or abandoned so that we could keep enjoying our peace and prosperity. Most people did not know that the PM and his advisors thought that with our Military might would make sure that we had a quick victory.

Most people also did not know that some special forces were being raised that were equipped with alien weapons and enemy detection systems. There was nothing that would be able to counter that. With all this it was inevitable that we would attack our neighbours.

CHAPTER 12

The Zotharians

The Scouts Markov and Zetas were jubilant that they had successfully paved the way for the landings and felt rewarded because they were instructed to the only Zotharians to be in contact with the Indian humans. The first six outposts and the three larger population domes were polulated. The leader of this earth colony was also happy that they were so easily able to build the domes and start sending back kutudge (grass) so essential for recovering their seas and this had a direct impact on their atmosphere.

What they were giving to the humans was insignificant. If things continued like this the faction back home that wanted a full-scale invasion and full colonisation of this planet would be defeated and the peaceful faction would prevail. The more Morkov and Zetas studied these people, the more they liked them. Most of these people were friendly and devoted to their families and Gods. The reason for selecting them now also became a reason to like them. Markov's reports to the home planet made it clear that it was in the interest of Zothar that they support this country and make them dominate the world; these would be the least difficult way to protect the interests of the home planet and fulfilling its survival needs. The Zotharians had tried the direct attack and enslavement on two planets before this, and the wars and subsequent rebellions were costly and complicated and finally resulted in the complete destruction of the worlds.

The experiment on earth would work well with the present strategy unless the hotheads back home came to power. As things stood, we had achieved our goals quickly by first bio implanting 29 females of the species. The leader who became their supreme leader volunteered for an implant when told that it would be easier to communicate with him. All 30 made it easy for us to implant another 3000 people spread all over the country and in every organisation. We could do it without transporting them to our ships by momentarily rendering them unconscious at their meetings. These implants were necessary to help support the school of thought in a majority of these people, which was in our favour. What was in our favour was that people here support their governments' plans that allowed us to set up our domes here. Also, we could use these people to quell resistance to us if it ever arose.

Everything was going well and we were lucky that these humans were not very demanding. It was easy for us to please them. Once the population domes were in place, we moved a large number of our people to these three domes. One fourth of the population still alive were now on earth.

These humans could never be allowed to find out about the disaster that had befallen our race. All our technology was not helping save us from the damage we had caused to ourselves. That was the reason that we told the humans nothing about us. The advantages of dealing with people like these were that they had a lot of expectations. Our arrival had brought them prosperity and growth and this was visible to all of them. They would never want to displease us. Our bioimplants helped us to monitor them, so we knew that there was no danger.

We would have to make more domes so that our entire population could be moved to earth before bioengineering could be done to recover our planet's atmosphere. Back at our planet, some felt it would be better to start again on Earth after altering its atmosphere, but this was challenging and expensive. The point of view of the peace loving people to prevail. These people were clear that the move to Earth would be for as long as it took for the Zothar planet back to what it used to be and this would be easy because of what we could easily get from Earth.

It was hard for the Scout-ambassadors to get sanction from the home planet to assist in helping India to eradicate the nuclear arsenals. The permission came because the dangers of such weapons to Zotharians on Earth. The home planet would have like to destroy such weapons on all earth but would do so only if the earth partners suggested it. The earth supreme leader did not want to provoke the Western powers at this time and wanted the advantages to trade with them.

The Zotharians keenly observed these Earth people and were puzzled by the numerous Gods and languages. Back home they had grown to a point where one word was found useful rather than the five languages that they had hundreds of years ago. These people were so different that it was good that we were not allowing our people to mix with them. We used the unbreathable atmosphere as an excuse to deter any curious Zotharians from wanting to venture out. We had come across sentient beings after thousands of years, and there was considerable curiosity, taken care of by giving our people enough to watch on their reality screens. Our reality screens were three dimensional and offered sight and smell and feel so our people got to experience these humans.

The Earth people were equally curious about us, but their leaders had managed to take care of it using the excuse of our poisonous atmosphere and another original one was that we would be invisible to humans. It seemed to have worked since there were no requests from the earth people to meet ours. The meeting of the Scout Ambassadors with their supreme leader was enough.

We had encouraged the Indian leaders to make their country stronger and for this purpose, we had asked them to expand their boundaries. They were very reluctant but, in the end, their greed for advanced weapons and the lure that we would require more land worked. We were interested in their territorial expansion because we perceived threats from these places. We felt that these places could be used by other countries to cause strife in our new home on earth. This expansion was a preventive measure.

With our long life spans, we were a very patient people and hence our slow colonisation of this place. The plans our leaders made would be implemented slowly and would escape notice and controversy. We had established a good and smooth working relationship with these people and would keep it like that.

We had influenced our earth friends to expand their boundaries and for this, they would require our help. There had to be enough people in those countries who would welcome them create positive feelings for the invader. People there were identified and fitted with bio implants. The people in the northwest country were influenced more by the religious leaders and manipulators from their intelligence services. So such influencers were teleported to our scout ship, implanted and sent back. We inserted 30 such people there. Soon they expanded their already big circle of influence, and it grew to a significant size. We would activate this network of support when the time was right.

CHAPTER 13

More from the Masters

One night in my dream state I was back with the masters. For the first time, the other members of the group of thirteen were also there. I wondered what surprise was in the offing. All of us looked at each other and waited. Om spoke "we have finally made contact with the Zotharians; yes that is what they call themselves. The news is good and bad. But first I must confess that what we picked up from the minds of these people, perhaps due to their fear, was hostility. Their initial plans were warlike based on their studies of humanity. Lucky for us this race has a long life span and wisdom and patience rule. Before launching an attack, they looked for an easier way. For the aliens, the easy was one where there would be none or little loss of life." He said. "After observation of Indian people and their aspirations, they adopted a more liberal strategy." "We have nothing to fear from them for now, but we must continue to be vigilant because there is a faction of the Zotharians who are destructive,"

Om told us that the Zotharians had a huge group of people in their spell and for now these people were being used positively. But they were pawns and pawns could be used both for good and bad. Our group was asked to do nothing for now, and the masters would tell us what to do. We would be strengthened spiritually and raised to a level where we would be able to communicate with anyone telepathically and also influence through this medium. The Zotharians knew about the Guardians and their leaders in home planet had been had been contacted by the Guardians telepathically. The Zotharians respected beings like the guardians because they too had Guardians watching out for them. As long as guardians from both the planets prevailed these races would live peacefully.

The next day all of us met again and this time, there was a relief. Our fear was gone, and we felt right to be a part of the guardians. We wanted to start work on developing our self as quickly as we could. I felt that we should also ask our spouses to develop themselves without telling them about the Guardians or the aliens.

My next meeting with the masters happened much sooner than I expected. Om had something special to say me, and when he did, it shook me up. They had discovered that Mansi and others had been implanted with a special bio-implant and were carrying out all he activities on their behalf. So far nothing dangerous to humanity but needed to be watched and so did the other girls. He said that my proximity to Mansi would make it easy to keep an eye on her. For me, this was terrible it because I loved my wife a lot and this could jeopardise our relationship.

The next morning she brought me a cup of tea as I was getting out of bed. "Are you OK?" she asked. I wondered what she had seen on my face and said: "I'm fine". We went about our usual routine, and I was quiet. I was feeling uncomfortable, and I was happy to escape to my office. It was difficult for me to concentrate on work and had a throbbing headache all day. I wondered how I could keep an eye on Mansi When she was not with me. The evening came, and I was reluctant to home. I kept dawdling in the office until I got a call from her. When I reached home, she made me welcome in particular and made a very special meal for me. She was the seductive wife, but it was only making me suspicious. It was not a good evening and ended up with her crying and me getting angry. I wished I had never known about her; we had been so good together. Life was becoming unbearable, and I was not able to handle it anymore. I had to talk to someone.

Sleep took me again to the guardians. Om looked at me with profound compassion and said "Mansi has no idea what has happened to her. She deserves your compassion and support and not your suspicion. You're keeping a watch on her is for her protection and not to catch a criminal. She is not a criminal". His words made me see things differently, and I was not upset anymore. I went home and apologised to Mansi telling her that I was tense about a case and hence was behaving badly. Life at home became normal after that. It was like a second honeymoon. We were going out every second day and making love every day.

I had decided to put a tail on Mansi and all the TA's in my jurisdiction and requested Kishore to do it in other areas, so all 29 girls were covered. The operatives were asked to report everything they observed and had nothing even after even six months, and we were uncertain if we should go on. So after another two months, we stopped.

The next five months passed blissfully with me as the protector of my beautiful wife. Life was as normal as possible. We were happy. Until one day something happened that I shattered our idyllic existence.

I got called in the middle of the night. "Anil sir, please report to HQ right away, there have been explosions all over the city and in Delhi and Kolkata too" spoke the breathless voice of my duty officer. I rushed to HQ and on the way I could see groups of people gathered on the roads, a sight unusual at such a late hour. There was bedlam at HQ, and when I entered the control room, I saw the chief there. "Come to my room," he said and propelled me in that direction. "There were simultaneous explosions in six locations, The Naval Dockyard, the airport, Mumbai Central Railway station, one outside the CM's residence, one at B.A.R.C and one at V.T station. It looks like these were carried out by suicide bombers. There were four explosions in Delhi, one at the air force station Palam, and another at New Delhi Railway station and one at Police Headquarters. We know that Kolkata has also had explosions, but we do not have the details yet. "He said. I had never seen him so angry in all the years we had known each other. "Curfew has been declared, and the announcements are being made now on radio and television. We have to deploy loudspeaker equipped vans to start patrolling different parts of town and make announcements."

The next week was hectic. We had to apprehend the perpetrators of these blasts. Our informer network all over the country was questioned about anything suspicious they had seen. Many leads were given, but we still had no clue. Finally, a call was intercepted, and it took us to a Kolkata suburb. A man was found there and under sustained interrogation revealed the plot. It took another week, and we found all except one terrorist. One had managed to get of the country. There was no doubt about the people behind these bombings.

Protests were lodged with our neighbour, and they vehemently denied any involvement as they had always done. This time, we were all hoping that the government would solve this problem once for all.

Intelligence intercepts also indicated that there were more bombers here and in other cities too. Forces all over India were on alert. I was asked to coordinate with the Army and also supervise south Delhi and Cantonment as per plans that had already been often drilled. The army, now on full alert apprehended two bombers and killed them before they could detonate themselves. Two explosions happened, one in Pune at the cantonment and another in Bangalore, also at the cantonment. The dome in Kutch was targeted, but the bombers could not get past the alien defences.

A state of emergency was declared by morning, and a special session of the parliament was called the next day. The nation was enraged, and many angry members of parliament demanded action. There were many who felt that we should find a diplomatic solution. Most people believed that such solutions usually resulted in empty promises and wanted something concrete to be done. Since there was enough evidence that the bombers had come from across the border, our Prime Minister took the decision to declare war on Pakistan.

CHAPTER 14

War

The armed forces of India were waiting for such an opportunity and lost no time in launching the offensive. We needed an excuse to attack, and now we had one. The explosions happened on Monday night and Tuesday evening just before sunset; our air force carried our simultaneous strikes on all enemy airfields and all known ordinance depots and fuel storage depots across the border. All known radar installations were also knocked down. Their anti-aircraft batteries managed to destroy two of our fighters. They were completely taken by surprise because such retaliation by India was totally unexpected.

What were even more unexpected were the multipronged attacks launched by the Indian Army at midnight. There was an attack from the Lahore sector, another from the Sialkot sector and one from Rajasthan. There was a seaborne attack on Karachi. Under cover of bombardments from our ships, our troops secured Karachi. We dropped paratroopers at strategic locations and paved the way for the landings. Our naval aviation and submarines dealt with some initial resistance from their Navy but the surprise was on our side, and our victory in that sector was swift and decisive.

Tank regiments and the Special Forces equipped with the powerful alien weapons lead the assaults. They pushed forward before the enemy could realize what was happening. We captured Lahore by Wednesday morning

By the time our multi-pronged attacks started, Paratroopers were dropped on all known military installations in Pakistan. There was fierce resistance and with support from the air, these facilities were secured. Afer that reinforcements and supplies were landed. The ensuing chaos made their defence in all sectors inadequate.

Frantic calls made by the US president to our PM, but he was not available. Similar attempts by other world leaders also failed. Our PM did not want to speak to anyone at this time. This time, the gains made by the sacrifices made by our soldiers were not going to be given away because of international pressure.

Our forces were facing fierce resistance but were pressing on. Speed was the key and despite all the resistance almost all their cities had fallen. Their army was getting pushed back. Our strategy had our troops just go around civilian areas so that no time was lost securing the cities. Our military would surround them; leave a force to let no one in or out and press on. We had enough paramilitary forces that to deployed around their cities. Any troops left inside were dormant or surrendered. If they did not our helicopter gunships were used against them and they soon laid down arms.

Out Navy had put a virtual shield in the seas around the country so that any threat from that direction wa contained. This pre-emptive planning proved useful because while our army was advancing on the western front, the Chinese Navy attacked our fleet in the Bay of Bengal. We lost one destroyer and one frigate, they lost two destroyers and submarine and a battleship and stopped them. We had the Chinese attack but not so soon. They also launched missiles at are major cities, but they could not get through our alien supplied air defence shield. We did not retaliate because we did not want war with them.

There was jubilation everywhere in India. Finally after three decades, we were doing something after getting so many pin pricks from across the border. The civilian populations would greet our soldiers with flowers wherever they saw them.

I and all my staff, as well as those of all police forces in the country, were on high alert. There were chances that some internal elements may try sabotage.

The public irrespective of their religious beliefs stood behind the country and its leaders. The people wanted lasting peace and were willing to support the governments' efforts to secure it. The spirits of the population were high even though there were many families had lost loved ones.

A call by our PM to the Chinese premier made it clear that any further act of war against us would call for retaliation. We had restrained our self for now and would not tolerate any more provocation. We explicitly told them that they should not view our restraint as weakness. We had no intention to have war with China, but if they continued to provoke us, we would have no qualms about attacking them too. They were aware of our military strength and our resolve and asked their forces to stand down. They were also mindful of the fact that the aliens were on our side, and so was every civilised country in the world.

The US president was informed that we had declared war and the reasons for it after a significant amount of territory of Pakistan had been overrun. It was not a surprise when the US president offered assistance to deal with the Chinese if required. So the Chinese managed to help us get US support by attacking us. Our strategy was working.

Frantic efforts by the Pakistani government for help were falling on deaf ears. The world did not have any sympathy for a nation known to be a launch pad for terrorists. The recent suicide bombings on our cities had been reported worldwide, and the world was on our side. The UN suggested that they send a peacekeeping force, but this offer was declined. India made it clear that India had annexed Pakistan, and our troops would not withdraw. The people were now Indian citizens and would enjoy that status.

It took fifteen days of hard fighting before many units of their Army surrendered. This was less than half their army. The rest of the military fled into Afghanistan and continued to launch attacks against our forces from there.

In spite of all precautions, suicide bombers managed to sneak in and carried out attacks here in our cities and also at our army posts in Pakistan. Many lives were lost in our towns, unfortunately, all of them civilians. It was hard to restrain our soldiers from carrying out atrocities against civilians in enemy territory. Fortunately, only a few such incidents took place and perpetrators were brought to book. There was an uprising in Kashmir and that was put down quickly. Without support from Pakistan, Kashmiri militants could not sustain a fight with the army.

I was busy night and day dealing with the suicide bombings and coordinating pre-emptive actions to ensure that more such attacks did not happen. I had not been home for a week and managed to speak to my wife Mansi only twice. She kept herself busy with her group; they were supporting families who had been affected by the bombings.

The government of Pakistan finally surrendered and appealed to the rest of their armed forces to surrender for the sake of their families resulting in many more army corps putting down their arms. All military installations were under our control now, and it was only the army holed up in Afghanistan that was causing trouble.

The Afghan government expressed its helplessness in dealing with the Pakistani soldiers even though they were not happy to have them on their soil. India got permission for Indian troops to enter and engage the remnants of the Pak army. The moment the Indian army carried out these attacks, there was rebellion in Afghanistan. The government was ousted and a militant group took control. These militants gave full support to the remnants of the Pakistani army and their ranks were further supplemented by mujahideen from other Muslim countries.

Our planners had foreseen this and had made plans to deal with this eventuality. A special AF-force of five army divisions was ready and was at the Afghan borders in ten days. These were special mountain divisions with fierce Gurkha and Sikh soldiers. Centuries ago the Sikhs under the reign of Maharaja Ranjit Singh were the only ones to subdue the Afghans and were feared by them.

We declined support offered by the US and others. We also made it clear that we had no plans to expand further. We had friendly relations with Iran, and they had nothing to fear from us as long as they did not support the rebels. We warned them that we would not tolerate any surreptitious support to the rebels.

Our strategy to win the fight in Afghanistan was to concentrate on making sure that military supplies did not get into the country. We made sure that nothing would get in from either Pakistan or Iran. We landed forces on the Iran-Afghan border. We used drones extensively and managed a complete blockade. Tajikistan, Turkmenistan, and Uzbekistan were proving to be a problem. We sent one of our special divisions there and with the alien detection systems and weapons they were able to limit military supply smuggling to a minimum.

Our groups massed on the Afghan border soon neutralized the Pakistani army hiding there. Many surrendered and a lot died fighting. The loss of life on both sides was high, and it was sad that had to fight them at all. We did not go after the Afghan rebels and chose to negotiate with them.

The civilian population was getting affected so we sent in supplies for them. Our army went in with the supply convoys in sufficient force and air cover that they were able to repulse any attack. Here again, without the support from Pakistan the Afghan people soon surrendered and the county was under our control. The rebels gave some trouble but our negotiations quickly won them over. The good amount of gold given to them made it easy. India had a lot of good will in these parts and the neutralization of Pakistan won us some respect from these tough people and that was also a mitigating factor.

The Alien Scout Ambassadors were happy that none of their domes had been threatened yet and their supply ships continued to go back with their agriculture produce and bring back platinum and gold. They had also brought in 100 tons of copper. For the first time, they gave hand held laser weapons. Ten thousand pieces were delivered for use by our special forces.

In the meantime, our administrators started work to restore Pakistan to normalcy. Locals were asked to cultivate the special grasses and the alien foods. This quick growing produce was bought by us at good prices and bartered as usual with the Zotharians. We provided funds for setting up industries there. The local administration indicted the local senior civil officials.

This and a lot of financial aid given brought life back to normal quickly. Our plan was to bring the same level of prosperity here as there were in the rest of the country.

Our laws were fully applicable here. Courts and police started functioning. Slowly people here began to realize that we were not the enemy. We spoke the same language, liked the same music, and shared a common history. We took pains to ensure that they did not feel like an occupied country. There was a large number of religious leadership here that had started influencing people to cooperate with the administration. Soon a semblance of normalcy was achieved.

When the aliens asked us to permit a big dome in Pakistan we felt relieved because they would do this only when they felt safe, and so did we.

Our group of thirteen was watching events carefully and so were the guardians. All of us were pleased that peace had finally come to the region. Peace at a cost much less than expected. We lost 1600 soldiers and the enemy lost 3000.

I took charge of policing this new area and moved with Mansi and my mother to Lahore because it was made the regional headquarter. My mom was very happy to be back to a place where she had spent her childhood before the partition of India. I was pleased that she was staying with us. She had never liked Mumbai, and that is why she had lived in Dehradun.

The new assignment brought new responsibilities. I had the job of setting up the entire police machinery. Most of my time was spent screening people from the old police force to decide who was suitable to join us.

Kavita came and visited us often and so did many of the others of our select group. Srini came thrice for his music shows. Gurjeet decided to start an industry here in Lahore; he bought back his ancestral home from where his family had to flee during the partition. Kishore came as a part of his duties, and he and I had to work closely to set up the intelligence network.

The work to set up the area to accommodate the new big dome began and I and my team had to ensure security for the township. Since the township was near Karachi, I was a frequent visitor, and I also decided to tackle the local mafia. This mafia was perceived as a threat and had to be neutralized. This perception was due to intelligence reports and was confirmed when one of the site managers was murdered. Our local police seemed jittery and I could see that there was no real effort being made to investigate this crime. When confronted, I was told that for years things were under control because the police did not take on the local mafia don who were politically well-connected and very powerful.

I decided to visit this person.

CHAPTER 15

Challenges

I went into the big house of the don. He stood up to greet me with a smile. A portly man with a handlebar moustache, he stood nonchalantly. As a police chief, I was accustomed to being greeted with some trepidation. "Salaam sahib, welcome to my home. What can I do for you?" he said and indicated to a servant who got me a cool glass of water.

I looked at him, and I wondered where all this confidence was coming from. I had used silence very efficiently, and I used it now. He filled in the silence, saying "What brings you to the home of a humble businessman? May I offer you a drink? I shook my head to indicate no and said "Mr. Qureshi, my staff tells me that I should have an understanding with you if things are to move smoothly here. I have come to inform you that I will not allow you to run your kingdom here. I know that you have both legitimate and illegitimate businesses, and I suggest that you stick to the legal ones from now on" I said sternly.

He very patiently explained that he had been influencing many things here, and things were such that it was not possible to wind them up quickly. He said "I understand things will be different now that we have new masters, but most people have benefitted by working with me. You can define the boundaries, and I will assure you that I will not cross them." He looked like a reasonable fellow, so I thought of making him our ally. I said "Mr. Qureshi, as you are aware there are many opportunities and I will help you get them if you are willing to be legitimate. I require that there should be no incidents again at any government site. When you have enough legitimate business, you may not want to continue with other activities." He nodded his acceptance and we shook hands. He looked like a resourceful man and could prove to be useful, I thought. I was proved right.

We did not have any more incidents at the new big dome location. Work went on as scheduled. One day I got a call from Qureshi at my Lahore office. He wanted to discuss something that he would not discuss on the phone. I asked him to come over and was surprised when he stepped in within the hour.

He looked tense and agitated, so I let him settle down and gave him a glass of water. He looked around and asked me if I could accompany him because he was afraid to speak for fear that my office may be tapped. My curiosity aroused, I went out with him, and we walked to a nearby children park. It was full of noisy children, and I was sure the noise would prevent any eavesdropping.

Qureshi spoke softly "My old contact from the CIA has been to see me, sir. These American's are unto mischief and are asking for my help. I thought you should know." He and kept looking was very uncomfortable and kept looking over his shoulder. "Please promise me your protecting sir; I do not want to get involved with these people. If I do I will have to break my promise to you, "he said. "They are asking too many questions about the site and want my help to sneak someone in; if not that they wish to put some surveillance equipment inside." I thanked him as told him that he should string him along. I asked him to tell me the identity of the person so that we could put him under surveillance.

On returning to Karachi, he informed my local person about the next meeting with the agent and my people were brought in place. After the meeting, the agent was picked up and locked up until I reached Karachi. I met him four days after his incarceration and was not surprised when he blustered "Mr. Anil Khatri, on what charge am I being held?" "Who are you? And what are you doing in Karachi?" I said. "I don't have to tell you anything. I am an American citizen, and I want to speak to my embassy." "Look, mister, you know who I am and I don't know who you are so if you have nothing to hide, tell me who you are? My men did not find your passport, and it is illegal to be here without papers. Let me know when you are ready to talk" I said and walked out. I asked my people to keep him locked up and well fed.

It took four days before he consented to talk. When he did, he gave me a cock and bull story. "My name is Smith, and I am a business man. I am exploring business possibilities in Karachi," he said. The passport had gone lost he said. I spoke to Kishore from the IB, who agreed to come and see our captive. He saw him through the one-way observation glass and immediately recognised the CIA man. When Kishore confronted him, he had no choice. He and Kishore had worked on an assignment in Delhi many years ago. Kishore assured him that he would be released if he would tell us what he was doing here; after all, we were a friendly nation so why hide things from us? He was willing to talk and told us that his government was desperate to make contact with the aliens or, at least, get some information. Smith had the audacity to suggest that their government would offer a great deal if we could help him.

Such attempts had been made before and our government policy was to let such agents go with a warning. We informed HO about this incident before releasing Smith. We were surprised to be told that we should hold on to him. It turned out that in the last 15 days there had been 12 such attempts, the latest being "Mr. Smith". All of them had been apprehended mostly because of the alien detection devices at the domes. The attempt in Karachi was to put someone inside before the dome came up.

A few days later our PM made a call to the US president. After the preliminaries, he said, "We have had a good relationship with your country for many years now and we not like this relationship to be jeopardised. Despite our requests, your CIA has made repeated attempts to break into the alien domes. They want to be undisturbed and we are responsible for ensuring this." The American President was silent so he continued. "We have 12 of your agents in custody. If you deny that they are yours, we will execute them". The US President had no choice but to stall and he said he would revert to a few hours. When he did, he was apologetic and asked for the release of these men. It was denied and he was told: "we will treat them well and we will not execute them unless another attempt is made by your people". There was no more discussion about this topic.

There was now some doubt about their intentions so our intelligence apparatus was put on high alert. There was no action by the Americans but China started massing troops on all their borders with us. A showdown was imminent and it happened in mid-summer. Our alert and strong armed forces foiled the first incursion.

It arrived in Bhutan. Within minutes of their attack, our air force went into action and destroyed all their supply lines to begin with. There were fierce battles with their fighters in the air with heavy losses on each side. Our forces had the means and the resolve, and they fought on. On land, the enemy had gained a foothold by sheer weight of numbers, but to counter that a full division of paratroopers was landed behind them. Their forces were surrounded and pounded from the air and ground. They were fierce fighters and determined to win. They could have held on until reinforcements arrived but we fielded 5000 fighters equipped with the new handheld weapons. This turned the tide. Simultaneously they ran out of ammunition because we had cut their supply lines. They surrendered after twenty days of fighting. We lost as many as 900 soldiers and they must have lost four times more. We disarmed them and sent them back. We did not want to take prisoners.

They were warned through diplomatic channels that in future, captured soldiers would not be returned. We had done it this time because we wanted China as a friend and not an enemy. They had not expected our victory and after this, their troops were withdrawn from our border. The show of strength had worked.

More satellites than usual were spotted high over India but we were smug that they would not see anything inside of the domes because of the green atmosphere. However the aliens were not happy with the probes from the satellites and all the electronics of these "birds" were fried by their weapons.

The state of the American economy was stagnant. India as a market for high technology products was now non-existent because we had access to alien technology that was far more advanced than any other country. They had to blame someone, and they did.

CHAPTER 16

Consolidation

A few months after our government in the new provinces of Pakistan had settled in I was ordered to attend a special meeting in Delhi. There were no details given except that this meeting may last for two days.

This session turned out to be so important that the Prime Minister and the Home Minister both presided over it. The purpose was declared right in the beginning. The PM said "The level of hostility by foreign countries is increasing to unprecedented levels. So far we have been fortunate that nobody has been able to cause any damage to our nation. However, we feel that our intelligence apparatus, as well as foreign intelligence, needs to be intensified. The good information helped us thwart the Chinese this time. The key factor was that we had correct information of their supply routes." he continued "we feel the need to strengthen the security apparatus and completely restructure it if need be. We will discuss and decide this by tomorrow evening."

This was perhaps the first time we had a meeting like this. It was clear that they wanted the involvement of a diverse group. There were people from the military, the police and intelligence services. The paramilitary forces were even included. There were two people seated behind the PM and introduced as the scout ambassadors. Their inclusion was a surprise and also an indication that the matter was serious enough to involve the Zotharians.

The importance of the Zotharians in our growth and welfare was well understood, but there had been a slight distrust so far. We knew now that we could trust them. I was not convinced about this but on the whole, people seemed comfortable.

The discussions had a clear objective. ABSOLUTE SECURITY OF OUR NATION AND THE ABILITY TO WIN ANY WAR. With this clarified, the officials kept their self-interest aside and discussed to find workable solutions. It was interesting to see that there no unnecessary arguments. The PM engaged himself in every discussion, and it helped that he had been the home minister before becoming the PM.

At the end of the meeting, it was decided that there would be one unified agency for internal and external security. It would aggressively gather intelligence internally and internally. It was named, Directorate of External and Domestic Intelligence (DEDI). Under this, there would be two divisions, just called internal intelligence division (IED) and the external intelligence division (EID). The names of the chiefs were announced, and it was declared that they would be given free reign and budgets that they required.

The DEDI head was Mr. Kishore, who was heading the IB for the last ten years, Mr. Pratap Veer was the head of the EID, he was the former head of RAW, I was surprised that I was named as the chief of the IED. I would be required to move to New Delhi our capital. It was a great responsibility, but It would be nice to work with Kishore as the boss. With the guardians to guide us, we could not go wrong.

Mansi was delighted to move to Delhi, and so was my mother. We were allocated a big bungalow, and the house seemed empty for only the three of us. Our servants moved with us and had ample living space in the quarters at the back of the house.

I was given three months to set up my directorate, and I went about it with a vengeance. All internal intelligence personnel from all agencies were transferred to the IED. I interviewed people from each organization in batches to get a good understanding of their working. Standard best practices were incorporated into our work doctrine. Even though we could now afford it, not much technology was being used. This was first corrected. We purchased the best electronic communication and surveillance equipment. All personnel had devices that would allow us to track them at all times. These devices were undetectable and had been donated by the aliens. We did not realize that they were the bio-implants.

Our operatives were assigned and there were three in each district of every state. Every one of them created a network of informers. There was virtually one informer in every street. We instructed the informers that if anything untoward happened they would be held responsible. This was the stick, and the carrot was that they got a small sum of money every month.

More than the money these small vendors felt privileged to be selected for such an important task. We had the funds because the government was convinced about investing in this pre-emptive measure.

During my regular meetings with Kishore, the boss and old friend, I got to know about developments in the EID. Mr. Veer, having for the first time in his career had got such a clear mandate and budget, brought about a radical change in the EID. He was a passionate, patriotic man who had risen from a front line field position and one of the few ego-less persons I had ever met. He was a bachelor in his early forties. A very simple man and lived for only two things. One his was his job, and the other was his practice of yoga and martial arts. He had mastered the Indian martial art of Kalaripayattu. This perhaps was why he was so fit.

He and I soon became friends, and I was fascinated by his ideas and what he was planning and what he had implemented so far. India had a massive influx of tourists; this increase was due to the curiosity of people abroad to get a look at the domes. The government was minting money from the permits issued, allowing visits to designated areas outside the cities where there were viewing platforms. At $50 each this was a significant source of revenue because we had an average of 1000 people coming every month. Mr. Pratap Veer had decided to recruit people from among these individuals. There was an interview process for granting these permits where a skilfully designed questionnaire had to be filled up. This helped identify suitable candidates. There was a mandatory medical check-up, during which the qualified candidates were implanted with the bio-implants during the blood test. The preferred candidates were female. These devices made it possible for the EID to communicate and influence them at a distance and they would willingly do what they were asked to do. The aliens provided the devices and communication equipment. This was one of his methods of expanding his foreign network. All other methods also involved the use of bio-implants.

I now understood and was frightened by my understanding of the bio-implants. I now knew how 29 people plus our prime minister had become agents of the Zotharians. I was aware that there were thousand more that had been implanted. The aliens were in full control of all of us..

CHAPTER 17

Growth

I was appalled that we were completely in the control of the aliens. I spoke to Mr. Kishore, and he was also equally concerned. Mr. Veer was not aware of this, and we decided to keep it that way, for now.

The next meeting of the thirteen took place. This session was the first meeting after the formation of the DEDI. We shared our concerns with them, and it turned out to a bitter one. There was a feeling that we had not done anything so far and allowed things to go out of hand.

Some of us felt that the coming of the aliens and the supposed "control" had been good for us. There were only benefits visible so far. The gold, platinum, copper and the energy generators that we got from the aliens fuelled our rapid growth. So much wealth and employment had been generated from the farming for export to the aliens. Barren lands had been reclaimed.

Internal dissent was non-existent. There had been no communal riots since the landings. Religious fundamentalism had ended. Industrial development was at its peak. We did not need to import anything. We were exporting far more than we had ever done. Since we did not need fossil fuels, we were exporting them. Our economy had stopped being affected by oil prices. Employment was there for all who wanted to work. The standard of living was better than ever before. Any idle person was utilised on the farms where free housing was provided by the state, and this encouraged people to move, resulting in the absence of slums.

Government Health services were world class even though they did not match private hospitals. Basic literacy had improved to 85%. The education provided was specific to jobs. Children chose future careers early and received education for the job they were to fill.

The migration from rural areas to cities had reduced to a trickle. Rural communities were no less than cities, with plenty of electricity and amenities earlier found only in the towns. Small rural based industries were encouraged by the easy availability of loans and advice for identifying and setting up such industries.

Our cities were clean and pollution free. The public transport system was excellent and plentiful. Vehicles were all electric. Intelligent planning and location of office areas and housing complexes had eased the load on the roads. Housing near workplaces was readily available and financial support available from the government for relocation. The government was clear that it saved in the long run.

All this was happening because of a new breed of imaginative and innovative government officers who were working hard. All government departments were result driven. Results got rewarded, and failure to deliver results earned their dismissal. In the initial years, a large number of indolent government servants lost their jobs. Efficient government machinery made it possible to bring down taxes. The standard of living was higher than ever before.

Another factor was that there was a stable government with ministers who were driven to produce results. The prime minister involved himself with every stage of planning and control; they had no choice about performing. "Perform or perish "was the slogan found in every department.

The Ganga was cleaned up, and so had the Yamuna River. The Yamuna that had become a stinking drain was a clean river, and people were seen boating on holidays.

The civic sense was being inculcated in schools, and it was mandatory for adults to go to a "Civic duties Class". A certificate would entitle a person for a monthly free pass on the local public transport system. if people failed to produce a certificate, they got no services at the government hospitals and their driving licences would not be renewed.

Leading people from the states of the erstwhile Pakistan and Afghanistan were brought to see the progress being made and work started to replicate it there. Within five years they would at par with the rest of India

These and many other great things happening in our country was the reason given by the pro aliens in our group for us not to worry. The other school of thought was that we should worry. With so many people in the control of the aliens, we would be at their mercy the day they decided to misuse their power over us.

It was for this reason that I did not use the bio-implants in my division, the IID. I also decided to lay the framework of a secret plan to counter the aliens should the need arise. I involved only Mr Kishore from our group of thirteen in this planning. We spent half a day every week discussing and making this pre-emptive plan. We also decided that the surveillance of the 29 TA's would continue.

However, it was impossible to deny that the aliens had done only good things for us so far, and they had kept to themselves. There was nothing to suggest that they meant any harm. All my operatives who were watching the PM also had nothing but good things to report about the actions of the PM.

There were ten domes in India, and two more had been sanctioned. The government had put a team of dedicated scientists to find out if any of these would harm our environment in the long run. The report would take six months.

The PM called the DEDI for a meeting. I wondered what had happened. He initially only praised all of us, he seemed to be acutely aware of all our actions so far. He looked at me and asked, "Why are you not using the bio-implants on your personnel?" I had no answer and told him that I would have it done. He insisted that this was essential, and I had no choice but to get it done.

He then informed us the real purpose of this meeting. He told us that we were now planning to annex Bangladesh, Myanmar and Sri Lanka and wanted to know if we had intelligence inputs for strategic use to our armed forces. The attacks were expected soon. He wanted me to keep my network alert in case the enemy tried some mischief here.

This declaration was not such a big surprise because this was expected. Mr. Veer was ready to give his inputs the next day. I needed a few days.

Within the next one month, all our preparations were made. We were ready for the attack. Then there was one thing reported by the EID that would have to be dealt with before we could launch our attack.

EID said that Chinese forces in large numbers had been moved to Myanmar border adjoining Bangladesh. There were two divisions and air squadrons located there. The Chinese navy was racing towards the Indian Ocean. Their ships were headed for Sri Lanka. Intelligence gathered by Mr. Veer indicated that the Sri Lankans feared an attack from India and had asked the Chinese for support, and so had the Military Junta of Myanmar. Our PM was clear that the Chinese were not to be allowed to prevail in these parts. There were also intelligence inputs suggesting that a pre-emptive attack by the Chinese would be launched to capture Bangladesh

In our DEID meeting with the PM, he informed us about the plans and insisted that we should secure all our military installations and the alien domes. The scout-ambassadors had been pressing him to secure these countries too.

This news about the impending Chinese attacks made us bring forward our plan.

CHAPTER 18

The Clash

The Prime Minister was happy. The new development on the Bangladesh- Myanmar border would give us an opportunity to manipulate the situation to our advantage. He gave a call to the PM of Bangladesh. When he was on the line greeted him "Salaamailikum Mr. PM, how are you "The Bangladesh PM was surprised to get a call from the PM but did not show it." I have news about some developments on your border and I wonder if you are aware of them?" said the Indian PM. "What has happened, my friend?" said Mr. Rehman, "Is there something that we should worry about?" "Yes, we are worried and so should you. There is a big concentration of Chinese troops on your border with Myanmar, are you aware of that?" said Mr. Suresh Kumar. There was silence at the other end of the line and then the Bangladesh PM said, "Please give me one hour and I will call you back"

The Indian PM did not have to wait for long. The Bangladesh PM called back to confirm that what we had communicated to him was true and he had put his army on alert. "Are you sure your army can take them on? We know that an attack is imminent. "Said the Indian PM. "There is a Chinese fleet heading into the Bay of Bengal" "we suspect that both of our countries are going to be attacked." The Bangladesh President asked for time to confer with his people and promised to revert. He did, quicker than expected. His cabinet and ministers were panicking and he requested help.

The PM immediately ordered three army divisions to the Bangladesh border with Myanmar. Our divisions on the border with Myanmar were already in full strength and ready to attack. Forward airfields had aircraft ready to attack.

At midnight on 14-15 August pre-emptive strikes were ordered against the Chinese forces deployed in Myanmar. Our air force had intelligence about troop and aircraft locations and pounded them non-stop. Paratroops were dropped behind enemy lines. Our intelligence operatives blew up bridges behind them. The army began attacks both from Bangladesh and our territories bordering Myanmar.

The Chinese fleet heading towards the Bay of Bengal was attacked by the Indian Navy and a battle raged in the sea. The Chinese Navy had turned out in strength. There was one aircraft carrier, fifteen Type 056 corvettes ten 054A frigates, twenty 052D destroyers, five submarines a hospital ship and five ships that looked like troop ships. The Indian fleet had tripled in size since the alien landings and we had two aircraft carriers, fifteen frigates, fifteen corvettes, twenty-six destroyers and ten nuclear submarines. We had enough reserves in the Bay of Bengal and also in the Arabian Sea.

Initially our planners felt that this fleet was headed towards Dhaka but once the Chinese vessels emerged from Strait of Malacca it was clear that their real destination was Sri Lanka. Our strategy was to allow them to be close enough to be attacked by our land based aircraft. So our Navy engaged them initially by coordinated submarine and air attacks from our aircraft carriers. We did not block their advance towards Sri Lanka but kept attacking them from the flanks and rear. Their strength was formidable yet we managed to destroy one frigate, two corvettes and two destroyers in the initial engagement. We lost six aircraft. Air attacks from their aircraft carrier destroyed two Indian frigates and one corvette.

The enemy was determined and continued forward. What they failed to realize was that another battle group from our western naval command was ready to intercept them. As soon as they were within range of our land-based aircraft launched a massive air attack against the Chinese fleet. High altitude bombers dropped heavy bombs that wreaked havoc. Aircraft from our aircraft carriers launched missiles. Our fleet destroyed half the Chinese fleet. The strength of our air force surprised them.

They were now between two strong Indian Naval battle fleets and outnumbered.

Communication with their Admiral gave an opportunity for them to withdraw peacefully. It took them thirty minutes to agree. Their fleet was allowed to steam away carefully shadowed to ensure they went out of our waters. This sea battle had lasted for five days.

The Indian Resurrection

Chinese armed forces attacked India in the North East. Air battles raged between the two forces. Chinese missiles targeted Delhi and other targets in North India but thanks to the superior air defence systems given to us by the aliens, only one of their missiles hit, and it hit a civilian area near the airport in Kolkata. We lost one hundred lives and around 300 were injured. Our country was outraged.

Air attacks on our forces managed to give us casualties until our air force started attacking the Chinese airfields from where these planes were coming; this turned into another fierce battle with our air force losing 25 aircraft.

We did not have many disruptive agents inside China hence could not cause any extra damage. We had not expected an all-out war but were prepared. The battle raged on. The morale of our forces was very high because of our victory in the Bay of Bengal.

We raised the matter in the United Nations and denounced Chinese aggression. We made it clear that China was the aggressor, and we had a right to defend our self. No one could dispute the fact that this was the third time that we had been attacked. We requested every other country to stay out of this fight because we did not want this conflict to escalate into a world war. However, we bought more ammunition and aircraft from the countries who could supply them. Money was not a problem. Even though we had enough to sustain us in this war, we did not want to get low on our reserves. We had a good excuse to add to our arsenal without arousing concern.

So far we had avoided any missile attacks on mainland China, and we used restraint because rocket attack inevitably results in civilian casualties. We informed The Chinese Embassy in Delhi of our intentions and told that we had no interest in attacking the Chinese mainland. We were defending our self from their attacks launched from Myanmar. Our PM gave the Chinese premier the same message.

In Myanmar, the Chinese Army and the Myanmar forces were being mauled by our army that had advanced deep into that country. The local people were supporting our troops. We sent many offers to the Chinese to cease fire and withdraw peacefully, but were refused. We prevented any reinforcements from arriving in Myanmar, at sea; our navy was giving their ship a pounding. They were stubborn and kept fighting. Eventually, they had to capitulate, and they did.

Twenty days had passed, and the Chinese premier asked for a cease-fire.

We agreed, and the Chinese troops withdrew from all fronts. Our forces occupied Myanmar, and the Military regime was compelled to surrender to our troops. Once again Burma, as it was called before, became a part of India.

We paid a heavy price. 1100 soldiers lost their lives. We lost five ships and two submarines. 45 fighter aircraft, 150 tanks and 16 helicopters were lost.

Our prime minister informed the nation about this triumph. It had proved to the world that India was a strong power and could not be messed with. Sri Lanka was given a choice. It could either accept an Indian Army and Naval base there to foil any future designs by China or other nations or be attacked by us. They accepted a peaceful solution. Two Army infantry divisions and one armoured division were stationed there. A full-fledged naval base was also set up. India was magnanimous with a massive aid package to this nation and promised protection from any enemies.

A few days after the end of the conflict our PM decide to visit Bangladesh. A high-powered delegation went with him. Their mission was simple. It was to ask them to become a part of the Indian Union. The people and the leadership were aware of the progress being made by India and also how much the people of Afghanistan and Pakistan had gained. They were also impressed by the way the people were being treated and how the old leadership and government had been integrated. They did not want to make an immediate decision because they feared a civil war.

Soon after the visit of the Indian delegation a referendum was held. There were many attempts to disrupt the referendum but, in the end, it was completed. The nation accepted the proposal to be a part of India. The role of a vast number of our agents in the country and also other who had been implanted had a major role to play.

The world was surprised by these developments, but there was no visible reaction. The three reasons for this were one that our PM had skilfully persuaded the USA that we were a good ally and would not go against them. The other was the speed of the developments in this region. The third was the strength of our forces and the restraint we had shown as victors. Emissaries came from the Nepalese government to know what India had in mind for them. They were assured that we had no designs on them but if they wanted they could be a part of our great nation. The Chinese influenced the Nepalese so they refused. We decided just to let them be.

These events were a surprise to most of our people because India had never been so aggressive in the past. This was their first experience a courageous leadership since Indira Gandhi. The people were proud of the nation. The aliens felt secure.

Once the conflict was over, two new special zones were announced and work commenced to accommodate two large domes. we located one in Myanmar and the other in Bangladesh. The work started on a war footing and engaged labour round the clock. The local people were delighted with the employment opportunity and the projects gave a boost to the local economies.

I set up temporary offices in Dhaka, Rangoon and Colombo from where I quickly wanted to set up my internal intelligence network. The EID had planted operatives there earlier and these quickly integrated into the IID and within a month we had a robust system with the bio-implants in place. These implants were proving to be boon in maintaining law and order because every one of the persons with the implant was able to influence thousands of people around them to follow the law and support the Indian government.

The integration of the administrative apparatus had a model to follow and quickly fell into place. Both these newcomers to the Indian Union started to experience unprecedented peace and prosperity. They looked upon us as benefactors and the aliens as deities who had come and given a boon to India.

Kishore and I had not met the thirteen for a long time, and we had not had a visitation from the Guardians either. We were in regular communication with each other and wondered why the Guardians were not in communication. A phone call to the others in our group revealed that none of them had been contacted. I was due for some leave and during this time I managed to meditate daily. On the fifth night, I was back in my dream world and found myself in front of the guardians.

The news that they had was not good. Om informed me that the aliens were pressuring Suresh to additional sanction domes. If these were sanctioned, it would double the number of domes in India. At present, there were the initial small domes in Orrisa, two in Tamilnadu, and two in Maharashtra and one in Kerala. The large domes were in Gujarat, Andhra Pradesh, Rann of Kutch, Myanmar and Bangladesh.

CHAPTER 19

Understanding

Knowing what was going on was giving me sleepless nights. I shared my news and concerns with Kishore and he was also very upset. The eleven domes that were there in the expanded country were not a problem but doubling the number would put a strain on us. At this time we did not have a clear idea of the time needed for the eleven new domes. Only the Prime minister would know that.

Soon we got news that the Prime Minister had asked for inquiries to be made at suitable locations. The criteria were proximity to the sea, distance from populated areas and enough land for the walled area, the housing townships and agricultural land. The PM wanted this information within six months; this gave us some relief because it seemed like the domes would take five years to come up.

The Prime minister was initially taken aback when the aliens had asked for setting up eleven large domes. When they gave him the details, he was relieved. These domes would have to be setup in the next seven years. The aliens had surveyed our coastal areas and according to them, we had the spaces that met the criteria. However, he had asked his staff to find out. He did not give details of the sites identified by the aliens so as to get another point of view.

Suresh Kumar was an intelligent man and his skill was the ability to get the best out of people. His two sons had both grown to become engineers and ran successful businesses. He learnt a lot from them. It was his elder son who had suggested that he should ask two separate people to do the same job and select the best output out of them. His wife was a quiet person who listened to his ideas without saying much. Her questions were insightful and opened up more avenues for him to inquire. He was enjoying the responsibility that went with his job and was determined to do much for his country that history would remember him. He saw the aliens as a means to achieve his goal for his country. He was very fond of the three people who headed his intelligence services and was not willing to trust anyone else. He was inspired by Pratap Veer and his commitment to Yoga and fitness and because of this he had engaged a Yoga trainer and never missed a session. The yoga teacher accompanied him everywhere. He was doing a good job as a Home minister with the ruling party. The arrival and contact of the alien scouts with him had helped him to his post of PM. He was just 50 years old.

He had slowly started persuading his elder son to join politics and win a seat in the next election. He wanted to prepare him to be the future prime minister of the country and carry forward his vision for the country. India had regained its glory and he would ensure that she would never lose her position in the world as had happened before. He was laying the foundation for that. He hoped that the aliens would continue to be as benign as they were now.

As a survivor, he knew that trusting the aliens had put him and his country in their power. The implants that were working for us today could be used against us tomorrow. He was now desperately seeking to find out any weakness of the aliens that could be leveraged to keep them in check. He wondered if his intelligence chiefs had the implant and resolved to find out. He did not know how because if they were implanted, they would never admit it. There was a possibility that they did not know themselves.

One day he called them for a meeting in his underground bunker to share his concerns with them. He started by telling them that he had an implant and had no way of knowing if the aliens were listening to this conversation. He then shared his fears about the aliens and then said "Do you remember that I asked you, Anil, why you had not implanted your operatives?" he said. Anil frankly told him why and also that all of his operatives had still not been implanted. Anil and Kishore did not talk about the group of thirteen and admitted their own fears about the aliens and assured the PM that they would try and find out if there was any weakness that could be exploited. Pratap felt that a secret cadre should be set up and trained. Men who were to be picked up from areas that was so remote that there would be no chance of bio-implants in them. They were clear and told the PM that even he would not know about them.

The PM hoped that he had taken the right steps and that this would remain hidden for the aliens. He set up his next meeting with the Zotharian scouts and informed them that the new domes would be sanctioned in six months. The scouts had become very friendly with him and had started to recognise his moods. They could sense that something was amiss. When asked he told them his concerns. The scouts looked at one another and a thought-communication passed between them. "We have to inform him." And they told him about their planet and their people.

They showed him images of their planet and explained what they had done to it. As a race they had been very aggressive and had warred with each other to the point that their planet was on the verge of being destroyed. The atmosphere was almost gone and they had to live in domes with artificial atmospheres. They had been using space travel for mining and in all their exploration Earth was the first planet that had what they needed for survival. This relationship was important to them and they had no intention of ruining it. The methods used here were used because they could see the same mistakes being repeated and the methods used on Earth wold ensure that it would not happen.

The scouts admitted that in the beginning their intentions were aggressive because they had no idea how the people of the Earth might react. That is why they were very careful about choosing the place for first contact. They had found Indians as the least aggressive and also sufficiently weak to be taken over with least resistance. They had detected that the aspirations of these people were very high and that would prove to be useful.

When the Zotharians were sure that aggression was unnecessary and that India could be a real ally, they decided to land the big domes. For the first time, the big domes brought females and children to earth. Finally, the Zotharians felt safe here. The Zotharians felt that it was possible to locate the entire population of their planet here temporarily until Zothar got repaired.

The control that they installed via the bio-implants was preventive in nature. This control was to prevent divisiveness from causing self-destruction. They admitted that there was a faction on Zothar who had wanted to enslave this planet but tragedy had made most people on Zothar more enlightened. They understood that if the old aggressive methods were used here, history would be repeated. They reiterated that their population needed to be temporarily resettled here before the work of repairing their own planet could begin. Ten years after the all the people of the home planet came here their own world would be fit for them to go back. The eleven more domes would make it possible. The scout-ambassadors also informed him of a decision made by their leaders at Zothar that put his mind at rest.

Suresh believed them and was relieved and happy. He shared the news with his trusted officers of the DEDI. All of them agreed that the aliens may be sincere and resolved that they should give and get as much help as possible. Acquiring technology from them would be of the highest priority. Especially because of the decision of the Zotharian leaders that had been communicated to the PM.

I was full of misgivings. These were shared by our group of thirteen. What if these domes were a Trojan horse? What if these aliens turned hostile? What if these implants made us susceptible to them if they decided to take us over? My wife

Mansi and all of her friends and all other TA's had no such misgivings. In fact, it seemed like their role was to dispel any misgivings that anyone may have.

The PM gave orders for a special force to be raised specially trained for alien threats.

CHAPTER 20

The Space Pilot

I was fresh out of high school and waiting to decide what to do next. My father Gurjeet Singh had a manufacturing business in Ludhiana. He made components for the energy generating sets that used alien technology. One morning we were having breakfast together enjoying my mother's parathas, and he said "Son, why don't you start coming to the factory with me and learn the ropes? After all, you have to be the boss one day." I was waiting, with some apprehension for this day to come. I had no desire to take charge of his boring business.

He saw the look in my face and said "Look, son, this business had fed our family ever since we came here after the partition, and I have no plan to wind it up just because you don't like it. I have been waiting for you to join me one day. Together we can build it the way you want." I looked at my father, and I did not know what to say to this man who loved me so much. I did not wish to hurt him, so I agreed to start going to the factory.

Our factory was spread over an acre of land and consisted of two sheds. One had the foundry and the other housed the machines for finishing the castings that came out of the foundry. The process was for me very straight forward and just involved dealing with the labour and small daily problems. It bored me, and I wondered how my father endured it. But still it fed us and kept in the lap of luxury.

Three weeks had passed going to the factory and back. My father was happy that he had someone to have lunch within the plant. He was happy, and I overheard him telling my mother. "Now that he is regularly coming to the factory he will come to like it. At least, he respects me enough to come daily."

The next morning before breakfast I was waiting, for my father to come down, reading the newspaper. I saw something in the newspaper that caught my attention. It was half page advertisement of the WSD (World Space Defenders), announcing that the new Space Corps was looking for young, intelligent and physically fit boys and girls to join the force. If selected, they would undertake a two-year classroom course followed by space flight training. At the end of the training, they would be awarded a Space flight, Engineering Degree. The salary scale was not very impressive but the adventure it offered was irresistible.

My father came down and saw the excitement on my face. He glanced at what I was looking at and said: "Do you want to go?" I nodded expecting an outburst and was surprised when he said: "I am happy that you wish to follow in your grandfathers' footsteps my son." My grandfather was the hero of the family. He was commanding a battalion of Indian Army infantry and had lost his life, fighting insurgents in Kashmir. My mother was upset that her only son was going to take such a hazardous career.

My application was accepted and passed the written examinations with ease. The other tests including the physicals were not easy, but I got through. I think my determination had something to do with it. When the selection letter came, I don't know who was happier, my father or I.

My parents saw me off at the railway station in Ludhiana and the same evening I arrived in New Delhi. At the bustling station, there was a big banner of the WSD, and I made my way to it. There were about twenty-five eager boys and girls there. All of us were formed up and taken to a bus waiting outside.

The ride was a long one and we soon found ourselves outside the city. The ride went on for an hour before were saw the gate of a compound in front of us. The bus entered and what I saw in front of me was a college campus. The big signboard proclaimed "Special College of Engineering". The bus stopped in front of the building, and we went inside.

A tall person in a uniform stood in front of the big hall that we entered. The insignia on his lapel said WSD and he had a clipboard in his hand. "I am the commanding officer of this training centre; my name is Rana Rathore, Welcome to the WSD. You are the three hundred candidates who made it through the tough entrance examination, four thousand applicants have done it. Congratulations. You are the first batch of space fighter pilots in the world. Three hundred candidates will be trained in this facility. The next two years you will work hard, harder than you have ever worked before. Your life will depend on what you learn and practice here. Every week there will be a test and if you fail you will be out of this program." he said. "You will join squads of nine and when I call your name, you will go to the place where your squad number displayed." He quickly oriented us to this facility telling us the locations of the cafeteria, the training rooms and the location of the space fighter hangars. A daily training schedule was handed over to us.

I moved to my squad when my name was called, I was in squad number 7. I looked around at my mates and introduced myself. There were four girls and five boys. Renu Sood from Mumbai was tall for a girl and was a fair skinned Punjabi. Anjali Sengupta was a Bengali girl, pctite and beautiful who kept smiling all the time. Jaya.T was from Chennai and was tall and well built. Sapna Mathur was from Lucknow and was the prettiest girl in the group. The five boys were Gaurav Kapoor from Gwalior, Karan Thakur from Bihar, Sarath Kumar from Hyderabad, Haider Kadri from Karachi and yours faithfully Santhok Singh.

When the squads were assembled, we were joined by our squad instructors who introduced themselves as officers on deputation form the air force. Our instructor was in his late twenties, Flt.Lt. Anil Sinha. As soon as he introduced himself he appointed Renu Sood as the squad commander and asked us to follow him to collect our kits.

One room with nine beds was assigned to each squad. I was surprised with this arrangement until our instructor told us that we were now one squad and we would train together and would fly together abroad the space fighter assigned to us. We had to get used to each other because we would be spending months together on this fighting craft where we would not get any privacy.

I was happy with the daily training schedule that had classes on technical subjects in the first half of the day and flight simulations during the second half. There were early morning fitness and unarmed combat sessions. We were expected to hit our beds at 10 pm and be up at 5 am. The high point of the week for all of us was the actual flight in a space fighter. We took turns at each past on the plane except the pilots post. We were becoming familiar with the craft that we would fly and were told that we would be flying the aircraft as soon as we passed the flight simulator tests.

Our group had two pranksters Haider and Anjali, who were always full of surprises. Once I found something squishy in my bed and sprang up in alarm. It turned out to be a rubber snake. Another time Gaurav came out of the bathroom with his face black form some prank soap that he had used. "Don't be so uptight yaar" when Gaurav got upset. Anjali kept trying to upset me with Sardarji jokes.

The camaraderie of the group was high, and we were determined that no one from our group would fail. We gave everything to support each other and were jubilant when each one of us was among the top twenty in the entire batch every week.

One day I saw Renu Sood walking all alone with her head down, so I went up to her. She had tears streaming down her face. "What happened?" I asked "Nothing," she said as she sobbed louder. "Come on buddy tells me what happened? I know you are not the type to cry - no reason." I said. "My father died last night; he had a heart attack. I have to go and be with the family. But if I go I will be out of the program, I don't know what to do?" "Have you asked the squad commander?" I asked. "No, I know he will say no," she said. "You will never know if you don't ask, so please ask him," I said. I went with her, and we both came back upset because the answer was no.

"We are a space force, my friends, we will be expected to be out in space for six months at a time, and we cannot be recalled very time there is a family situation. So better get used to it now. If you cannot do that, you will have to leave the program. However, I will organise a video call with your mother and family members. You cannot tell them where you are." said Anil Sinha. Renu got off her upset and spoke to her mother and brothers who understood why she would not be able to join them. They were proud to have a member of their family in the space force.

Our training was hectic and tiring but very challenging. In our simulated flights, each one was rotated and assessed in each post. Each of us was developing fast and was doing well on one thing or another. I was getting excellent marks as a pilot and navigator. Renu was also ranking high in these two skills. The others did not do so well as pilots or navigators but were all rated excellent on the guns. They were doing well on navigation and flying too but not as well as the two of us. Much to the chagrin of the boys in our squad, the girls did better at unarmed combat.

While we were bonding and learning to supplement our strengths and soft spots as a team we were also learning the same about our space fighter which would be our alternate home of the future. We learnt about the weapon systems. The gun mounts had powerful laser canon and were installed in a way that they covered the craft from every possible angle of approach. There was no blind area. Our visi screens gave us visibility in a similar fashion. The detection system would detect any enemy craft within thousand kilometres. The flight computers were very accurate and needed little manual intervention; once the gunner locked them on a target, they blasted it.

The force field was unyielding and made us nearly invincible. The weakness was that each hit heated up the shield, and this heat was dissipated by fins all around this beetle shaped craft. There was a limit to the amount of overheating the ship could take. We had to ensure that we evaded as many enemy blasts as possible. In our simulations, our ships would explode after fifteen blasts if they happened within five minutes. Our pilots' evasive skills and the skill of our gunners would keep us alive.

Two years passed quickly and by the end, we had passed out with flying colours. We were a skilled squad who cleared every test and simulated exercise. During the passing out ceremony, we got our certificates and felt very proud when the one-star circle was put on our shoulders. shoulder. We were now space lieutenants. After the passing, our ceremony we were given fifteen days leaves to be with our families after which we were to report to a space fighter base in Myanmar. All of us were looking forward to meeting each other quickly and taking our space fighter into space.

When I reached home, I was not prepared for the welcome that I got. My father, my mother and many of my school friends were there. "Welcome back my son," said my dad with tears rolling down his cheeks when I touched his feet and those of my mother. I felt great to be home and soon made up for all of my moms' cooking that I had missed. May girls who had never spoken to me in school wanted to meet me. Relatives who I had never met before came to meet me. Everyone wanted to know about the battleship I was flying. I had to explain that my bunch had been trained to fly the space fighters. The people who would fly the battleships were trained at another location.

The fifteen days soon passed and I headed to Delhi, to take a flight to Myanmar from the air force base. All members of our squad were there, and we greeted each other like long-lost brothers and sisters. What was interesting was that none of us had developed any romantic attachment with one another. To fight and to win was all that consumed us. We were the protectors of the human race had been dinned into us.

When we reached Myanmar, we were happy when we were told that we had been assigned a space fighter and were being sent off on a patrol mission. I thought we should have a name for our squad, and we all agreed that we would call our squad "The Shiva squad ". We would patrol close to the moon and attack any intruders who crossed it. Many of the squads from our batch would have to wait until more space fighters were ready to fly.

CHAPTER 21

Preparations

The Zotharians believed in pre-emptive planning and there was a possibility that their more aggressive brothers may take the power back in Zothar. Hence, the present liberal leadership in Zothar wanted to make sure that Earth could defend itself in the case of attack on them. They were grateful that Earth had given them a haven. The current Zotharian leadership felt that they had to protect earth because it had inadvertently helped them save the Zotharian race.

For that purpose, heavy defensive spaceship weapons would be given to Earth. In addition to this, a detection system to detect Zotharian vessels and more equipment for ground soldiers would be provided. In addition to this, technology would be transferred for the manufacture of energy generators, desalination plants, weapons and other devices.

The most important thing was that the control of the bio-implants was given to us. These implants could only be controlled by the controllers that were compatible with them and no one else would be able to take control. Many were under Zotharians control at this time and their control would be given to us when they left or if hostile Zotharians attacked.

The Zotharians also wanted to make India strong economically and industrially to be able to face any situation. The alien ships started to bring in minerals essential her on earth and also those that were needed for the manufacture of other Zothar machines. They were clear that in the event of some Zotharians being forced to make a home here on Earth, they would not be a burden.

The Zotharians also started to help India with technology that could be used by them for space travel. The first Earth spaceship was being built. It was large enough to carry smaller fighters and small mining ships. There was sufficient space to carry large cargoes. The alien technologies made it possible for such a massive vessel to be built and launched from Earth.

Manufacturing of fighter aircraft using the alien technology was started and aeroplanes have been constructed at a frantic pace. Civilian and other aircraft that so far had to use fossil fuels were phased out as soon as new replacements were ready. The manufacture of 25 space fighters was also begun. These would be used to form a defensive shield around the country. All these crafts had strong force fields similar to what the domes used.

I had the opportunity to visit the manufacturing plant where the space fighters were being manufactured. There were robot machines that made them; there was hardly any human required. I was told that this plant had the capacity to produce ten space fighters a month. At present its capacity was not fully utilised. A training facility to train pilots for this craft had already been set up and training had begun using simulators. Training on actual spacecraft would follow.

Two large landing zones were built for the Zotharian cargo ships that were bringing in minerals mined from other planets. Rocks with iron oxides were brought in huge quantities. Hydrogen sulphide suffocated their planet and they brought it here for extraction of hydrogen and sulphur. Hydrogen did not have much use for them but here it was necessary.

In the meantime work on establishing the new domes had progressed. Four years had passed since the scouts had requested the additional eleven dome sites. Six dome sites were ready and would soon be occupied. Construction of the other four sites was on schedule and should be ready for another three years.

There was a good demand for rare elements like cerium, yttrium, lanthanum and neodymium. There was also a need for ruthenium, rhodium, palladium, osmium, iridium. The aliens were able to get us sufficient quantities to more than compensate for all the building we were doing for them. We had tonnes of copper and also silver for export.

During my trips to many places around the country, I was amazed by the change in the country. It was sometimes hard to believe that this was the same place where I had grown up. There were changes happening that we thought would require a miracle to accomplish. It was a miracle that red tape and sloth had almost vanished from government departments. Corruption and tax evasion had dropped significantly.

India had now become a very popular destination for employment seekers. This added to the workload of our department because we were given the job of verifying their antecedents and keeping an eye on them later. Research and development, genetic and Nanotechnology were fields where many of these expatriates were employed and some of them were sensitive posts. When such candidates got these jobs we got them implanted with the bio-implants during their medical examinations.

Our Prime Minister had an ingenious solution for tackling our population problem. Families with two children got a subsidy of 25% of the tuition fee for their children. It was compulsory for families with four or more children to send one child to the armed forces. This, of course, depended on their suitability. These kids were put into special military schools and later inducted into the military. This education was free subject to the condition that they served in the armed forces for at least fifteen years.

Our agricultural production was at an all- time high and we were building up reserves of food grain and pulses to meet any eventualities. All this was possible because an extensive canal system that networked the country. These were mega projects that linked many of our rivers and gave employment to thousands of people.

Our food processing and preserving industries allowed for large quantities of food to be stored. Many of the north east states of India were the largest producers of these foods. The country had added hundreds of cold storage facilities and food grain warehouses. We would never have food shortages in our country.

We had started the manufacture of the energy generators and fossil fuel free electricity was replacing old power sources. All the equipment was protected and could not be copied. This kept India with the monopoly for this equipment.

The special force was a division strong. It was fully equipped with alien weaponry. They also had sufficient conventional weapons and ammunition. Each unit also had armoured flying platforms equipped with weapons that had unlimited range. They could carry 20 soldiers. This was the first of the Space Corp division. Another division was under formation. There was a plan to form five such divisions with 5000 troops in each.

Special satellites equipped with alien detection systems girdled the globe. These would prove useful if there was a threat. These birds had very powerful cameras and electronic spy systems with which we could keep a watch on other countries too. They also had artificial intelligence controlled laser guns and force shields to defend themselves.

We decided that we should start space exploration and with the new space ships at our disposal we were sure to explore uncharted territories with the cooperation of the Zotharians.

Another three years passed and all the eleven domes were ready. The last three got occupied and we were relieved that there would be no others. Now there were ten more years for our alien visitors to stay.

In our inner circle of thirteen and the circle of 4 that included the PM and members of the DEDI, there was growing restlessness. We hoped that the aliens would depart in peace and their more aggressive brethren would not be allowed to prevail.

We were all working hard to ensure that we learnt as much as we could from them. With their help, a lot of alien technology had been replicated and manufacture of many new products had happened. A unique product that had swept the domestic and export market was the alien technology air conditioner. This used a completely different system with eco-friendly gases. The personal mobile phones were using a mix of cell towers and satellites.

Social networks were stronger than ever had many innovative features that were not possible before. However virtual friendships were giving way to a personal meeting with people since transportation was easy and traffic jams were a thing of the past thanks to electronically controlled vehicles.

We were prepared for any eventuality. Our military might was second to none. Our four person think tank along with the two scout ambassadors had a meeting to discuss what lay ahead. We discussed various possibilities for the future. One positive point of view was that the Zotharians would go back, repopulate their planet. They would leave the two big domes as trading outposts. The others would be handed over as virtually impregnable military establishments for our army. Our trade and collaboration in space exploration would continue. Another scenario was that the aggressive and impatient Zotharians may take control and attack earth to completely colonise it. They would initially leave India in peace because of its defences and may attack other countries.

In case the second scenario happened, it would fall upon India to defend the rest of the planet. Till now all our planning was only to protect our self. Now we had to plan for planetary defence.

Keeping this in mind, the PM decided to raise 20 more divisions of the Space Corps that would be equipped for rapid deployment using our smaller spaceships. Each such spacecraft could carry 5000 men and other equipment. We had the resources to build two mighty battleships for our space defence and work was started on them.

The world was watching these new developments and when questioned, our PM was open to explain that we were preparing a planetary defence system.

The ruling party was still going strong and the opposition rarely had anything to oppose. Our PM and his party came back after every election. People were actually beginning to question if elections were necessary. The government was the most responsive that we had ever experienced. The law and order situation was excellent. The crime was negligible, mostly drunks making trouble or some domestic violence.

Another five years passed and then our scout ambassadors gave us some bad news. In two domes the aggressive group of Zotharians was inciting trouble and a sizable number of people were rallying to their point of view. The leaders of Zothar were reasoning with them and so far things had not been resolved. It seemed like the aggressive ones were planning to go back to their planet when it was restored and wanted the others to stay behind. Only those aligned with the aggressors would be allowed to return. The aggressive ones were getting stronger day by day.

We had to speed up our preparedness and had five to seven years to be ready. With the help from our alien friends, we built another ten space fighters for planetary defence. We stockpile ammunition and further built up reserves of food. Medical facilities were expanded to take care of casualties in case of war.

Another five years passed and our scout ambassadors announced that all of them could not leave. More than sixty percent of the alien population would leave and the rest would stay. In the last five years, the aliens had stockpiles enough rare minerals, gold, platinum and silver to be able to pay for what they required from us. Out PM assured them that they had paid enough for us to sustain their stay. But they insisted that they would not like our charity.

The aliens, who had to go, departed. It took them five months to go. It was quite a sight to see the huge pyramid shaped ships rising into the sky.

Our scout ambassadors were among those who stayed behind.

CHAPTER 22

The World Comes Together

A large part of the aliens had left to repopulate their planet. It had been brought back to normal with the material sent from earth. On Earth life continued as usual except for the preparations for the alien invasion that would come.

This fact was not known and did not affect the common man as he had no idea about what was happening. Life was better than ever before. For me, it was routine except that we were alert to pre-empt the incursion by any hostile aliens just as the scouts had done. We were aided now by devices provided by the scouts that would help us detect anyone who came out of the domes. We had enough of the devices to cover all eleven domes.

There were 12 domes available for our defence forces. We used only six for military purposes the rest for manufacturing space fighters and weapons for them. We the small domes located one in Orrisa, two in Tamilnadu, and two in Maharashtra and one in Kerala. The large ones we had were in Myanmar, Bangladesh, Andhra, Goa, Gujarat and the Rann of Kutch. The inside alien atmosphere neutralized according to the technical guidance provided to us. After that, the domes were fit for use. The townships outside the domes continued as before and continued to grow and process alien plants.

Once again our plan to have a child was put aside, much to the dismay of my mother who was very old now and wanted to see her grandchild before she passed away. Mansi did not want a child even though I was keen that we have one. We were happy and as close as any honeymoon couple. Perhaps we had so little time together that we were determined to make it the best.

Kishore and I decided to have a meeting of our group of thirteen. We briefed them about the developments and the plans. Most were happy that the friendly aliens had stayed behind. They felt that the hostile ones would not attack their kind. Some of us were afraid that the one who stayed behind could not be trusted. In the end, we decided to inform the Guardians and wait. We did not know at this time, that the time would soon come for the group to play their part.

There was a meeting of the DEDI with PM. He unveiled his plans to inform other nations about the likelihood of an alien attack and wanted to know if we had any concerns about it. The director of the EID told him that fear would be inevitable and also some hostility for us because we had been hosts to these aliens. They were unhappy that they had been excluded from any contact with them or given any information. On the other hand, they would be supportive because they respected us for putting an end to terrorism and had played a significant role in cleaning up the atmosphere of our planet. We were unanimous that the information about the bio-implants must be a secret.

A special meeting of the UN was requested citing reasons of matter that required urgent attention. Calls were made by our foreign ministry to ensure that all world leaders attended. Our PM gave details of what had happened. There was pandemonium, and it took some time for the order to return. "We pledge our space fighters to give you protection, but we cannot be sure that their ships will not get through. Those of you who have the means to fight can do so. Those who need our support will get it we must stand together and fight for our planet."

At the end of the session all nations had agreed that they should put their differences aside and have a joint action plan. They would return and send their military leadership to India to make a joint action plan.

Within a week, the senior most military personnel were in New Delhi. The initial meeting of 150 people realized that this was too large a group to plan strategy and hence Generals from the USA, UK, Germany, Russia, China and Japan and India were voted to make the world defence policy.

The group of seven settled down to draw up plans. Our Scout-ambassadors had given the alien point of view and estimated targets. According to them, Africa would be the initial alien target so that a foothold would be established and used as a launch pad. Multiple landing sites could be expected there deep in the jungles. The Strategic planning team decided that rapid deployment battalions stationed in many places across Africa. Missiles and fighter planes would be deployed to strengthen the air forces of African countries. Also, forces ready for rapid deployment would be on alert all over the world. Missile forces would be augmented and readied. There would be a unified command that would operate out of the dome in the Rann of Kutch. A communication network would connect all the forces. The scout ambassadors informed the planners through our PM that the aliens could knock out our wireless networks before the attacks so they would be rendered useless, a solution had for this must be found.

The scout ambassadors gave a viable solution. Bio-implanted personnel carrying special bio-implant like communication equipment based on each location. The communications through these devices could not be intercepted by anyone who did not have such a device. No one would know that the personnel were bio-implanted, this was top secret.

The command centre established. The communicators sent to various locations. Drills were regularly carried out for practicing operational scenarios.

Forces augmented, ammunition stocked and ready, civilian shelters established. Civilian volunteers trained and armed; Hospitals prepared for casualties. Adequate food and water stocks were available at population centres in case power was knocked out. The world was getting ready to face the enemy.

Our allies, the Zotharians used their equipment to keep an electronic eye on their home planet. They would give us an early warning, if possible. They had asked us to expect at least five large craft carrying fighters and 25000 soldiers. The fighters had the capacity to bombard us from outside our atmosphere.

The only spaceship that we had hid behind the moon. It carried ten space fighters and had powerful guns for attack and defence. We were hoping that it would stay undetected and attack the enemy from behind while our other forces engaged the fleet from the front. The element of surprise may perhaps help us.

The enemy was patient, and we waited for the attack that did not come. One year passed and then another. The world heaved a sigh of relief, and many governments felt that keeping their forces on alert for so long was a waste of resources. The central command warned that this may be the strategy of the enemy; to lull us into a state of complacency. The result was that surveillance of the skies continued and we waited, hoping that the attack would never come.

I decided to take a small vacation, and we travelled to my hometown, Dehradun to spend some time with each other. Mansi was very happy, and so was I. The future was uncertain but we both wanted to make the most of the time we had now. During our long walks together I discovered new facets of this wonderful girl whom I had married. More than ten years had passed since I found her under the strange circumstances. Whenever I broached the subject of a child, she would go silent. That was a topic she would always avoid.

During this short holiday I got some time to meditate and as usual, I had the dream where the Guardians spoke to me. They told me that what they had foreseen was going to happen soon, and our survival would be at stake. They were aware of the developments and the state of preparation. They still felt that we were in for a difficult time ahead.

We returned from our vacation and got back to work. Reports from my operatives did not indicate anything of concern. There was some apprehension about the imminent attack, and there were fears that the aliens here on earth may turn aggressive. A few demonstrations held in front of the PM's house. I liked the way our PM handled it. He called the leaders into his home and asked them why they had doubts about his good sense when he had never let them down. They had no answer and took their followers home.

We in India were resting easy under the impression that if the invasion came, India would not be the first attacked. The alien domes were here, and they were not likely to attack their kind. Our forces were ready to give help wherever in the world needed. What happened later was a surprise.

CHAPTER 23

War With The Invaders

It was a cold night in late December; it was the coldest winter we had ever experienced. It was one of the evenings when we both were at home. We had decided to go to bed early allowed our hormones to take over. Winter always had this effect on us. When we finally fell asleep, I was in the middle of a dream when I heard the telephone bell ringing.

It was my office informing me that the alien fleet was spotted and was approaching Earth fast. The DEID senior staff and their families were asked to accompany the PM and his team to the Orrisa dome headquarters right away. Mansi and I were ready for this eventually and we did not even have to pack. We picked up our bags and got into the waiting vehicle.

At the PM residence, everyone got into the waiting hello craft and we were whisked off to the dome. At the dome, the action was visible on big screens. The speed of the approaching fleet was astounding. They had gone past the moon already and would be here in minutes. It was a not known how they had escaped detection so far.

Our space fighters zoomed out and engaged them immediately. The five invader craft took positions around the earth atmosphere and disgorged smaller craft that engaged our fighters. Our strategy was to lure them closer to earth so that our stronger Earth batteries and missiles could pound them. This plan worked initially and seven intruders small craft were destroyed. In our dome, all that we could see was the coloured dots on the screen and some flashes when a spacecraft disintegrated.

Three of the big alien craft positioned themselves above India and their main laser cannons started firing at us. They were trying to destroy our aircraft on the ground. Fortunately, our battle plan had required these aircraft in the air as soon as the alien fleet was spotted. The aircraft survived but many military airfields destroyed. Our fighters would remain flying to intercept landing craft. The aliens also started attacking the domes where the earth based aliens were living. The high defences prevented any damage.

In the air, the battle raged and it looked like most of the alien forces were attacking India. There was no action in other sectors. We had to draw all our space fighters back to our space to ward of the enemy fighters. We had not even managed to put a dent in the big battleships. Our space fighters got mauled and had to withdraw closer to earth so that earth based guns could deal with the intruders.

All the observers in the PMs' dome were tense. Mansi and I were staring at the screens; it was the first time Mansi had seen anything like this. She did not take her eyes off the screen and neither did most people. It was hard to tell who was getting the most wins. Our boys in space were faring very well but many killed. For us, the life of these men and their spacecraft was very precious. Every craft lost brought us closer to losing our planet to the aliens. The thought of all of us becoming slaves was not a pleasant one.

The tide started turning when our battleship emerged from its hiding place behind the moon and attacked the alien fleet from behind. The main laser cannon and space fighters from the battleship managed to obliterate many of the enemy's small craft and One alien battleship badly damaged.

With a significant portion of our space air fleet engaged in the defence of our homeland, the aliens were able to penetrate the air shield over Africa and landed six of their craft in central Africa and established two landing sites. By the time our rapid action forces had reached the two landing sites, the aliens had established fortified perimeters. Fighter aircraft engaged the enemy on the ground with high losses of aircraft both to the alien aircraft and also to the ground defences. The battle on the field was fierce and with the enemy ships on the ground they used their laser canons to cause extensive damage.

The fighting over Indian skies raged on. Our battleship was proving to be stronger and was more aggressive. Our scout-ambassadors explained that they were careful because, in the case of severe damage, they would not find it easy to land because of the atmosphere. Their landing suits had a capacity of only ten hours before recharge. Our battleship focused all its resources on one of the alien battleships already damaged and soon it exploded in a massive explosion.

From the ground, we saw a tremendous flash of light. Transmissions from our aircraft confirmed that one of the enemy battleships was down. The scene inside our dome was of quiet activity. The military command coordinated from the dome in the Rann of Kutch. Here we were getting reports from various cities across the country. There had been no civilian damage so far. The aliens had not attacked any civilian centres and had concentrated on the airfields. Radio communication was disabled but was coming back online in India. The action over India seemed like a feint to facilitate the landings in Africa.

We had to damage more of the enemy battleships and the small space fighters were not being effective. There were requests from many pilots to carry out Kamikaze attacks but permission for this denied. The USA had prepared long-range missiles with nuclear warheads for such an eventuality. One of the alien battleships was in range. Our spacecraft moved to a safe distance and the missiles fired. Everyone waited with bated breath for the outcome.

Within minutes, there was a big flash and the battleship disintegrated. There were whoops of joy and all our hope raised. There were now only three enemy battleships left and they congregated over Africa. They had located the nuclear missile launched site and their laser cannons bombarded it. The site buried underground and was not damaged.

The Smaller craft was going down on African soil and the aliens established two more fortified landing sites. Our quick response teams had already started engaging them. There was design for the landing sites. They formed a large circle and it seemed that they were preparing space for the big battleships to land inside. When the friendly aliens had landed in India before we had made walled circular areas for their craft before in India and we knew what was going to happen.

Ground forces were instructed to destroy the landing sites at all cost. Reinforcements reached there along with battle tanks and a fierce battle raged. Stopping the aliens was essential. The South African army para-dropped two divisions of soldiers. Their air force supported by other allies kept bombing and strafing the aliens. The alien aircraft from the skies were diverted to support their ground troops and many Earth fighters lost but our sheer numbers were able to blast the alien craft from the skies.

One enemy battleship started to descend and was attacked by a nuclear missile. This time, they were prepared and the missile was destroyed minutes after it launched. Missiles from multiple locations launched and one of them got through. The alien ship blew up scattering debris over a large distance. There were now two enemy battleships left.

The aliens kept sneaking in smaller craft down to the landing zones. We destroyed many in the air but some got through. The situation on the ground was still not decisive and the battle raged on. We were well prepared and had numbers on our side. The enemy had superior weapons and air power. This airpower depleted now but they held on. Reinforcements for the aliens kept arriving in small numbers. Our forces were also growing and attacking the enemy from all sides.

Two days had passed and we were still not sure if we would be able to stop the battleships from landing. The only defence that could destroy the alien warships was our nuclear missiles.

The aliens were determined to establish a base on earth so they attacked again. This time, while one tried to land, the other hovered well above it and kept on destroying the missiles thrown at the ship that was descending. This maneuverer proved to be successful and despite all the efforts of the combined Earth defence forces, the battleship dropped down and a dome went up. The battleship in the air was brought down by our nuclear missiles.

It was a victory of sorts but we had failed to stop them from landing and establishing a dome. Knowing about their mind control bio-implant technology, we in India were very apprehensive about what would happen. We had to destroy the dome in Africa and ensure that no one got out. Earth defence forces got instructions to do this.

A video conference of all world leaders was held to confer about this situation. The United World Defence Force (UWDF) strongly suggested that a nuclear strike is used to destroy the dome in Africa. Permission to do this given.

Our ground force surrounding the aliens on land was asked to withdraw to a safe distance and a nuclear strike ordered. There were multiple missile strikes. The enemy dome got destroyed because the alien ship on land was not effective in neutralising multiple missiles. The rest of the alien craft were quickly finished off.

The world heaved a sigh of relief. We had won the battle but the cost was high. We were down to 22 space fighters. Our only battleship had five fighters left. Combined air forces had lost 600 aircraft. Ground casualties were massive and we still did not know the number of dead and injured. We had managed to save our self this time.

India had played a stellar role in its spacecraft and the world experienced its first battle with an alien race. We were lucky because the enemy force had not been very strong. It was possible that they did not expect this kind of opposition and had sent a smaller attack force. We had to become stronger.

The friendly alien Scout-ambassadors warned us to expect another attack. The Zotharians would go on fighting as long as the aggressive faction was in control and they were honour bound to avenge this defeat. The Zotharians now knew what they were up against and would come prepared. The silver lining was that the alien planet had revived recently and may not have developed a larger force at this time.

Our only hope was to take the fight to them if we had to survive. So the world would have to build up its forces to take on the Zotharians. I had to admire the strategic thinking of our Prime Minister, who declared that we should set up a secret base on Mars. Here we would assemble a fleet from where we could attack Zothar. He got the cooperation for the Local Zotharians to acquire blueprints for building the warp drives that would be needed. India and only a few people were aware of it. It was a tightly guarded secret.

Work began to mass-produce space fighters in India. If we worked on a war footing, we could manufacture 50 in a year. At least, a 200 were needed. To boost production, a part of the work was subcontracted to firms in China and South Korea. We decided to make the engines and laser cannon in India, final assembly done in our country. With this decision, it was estimated that the production could cross 75 per year. More battleships were needed, at least, twenty. They would have to be bigger to carry at least 25 space fighters each and 2000 soldiers. We equipped them with stronger laser cannons and nuclear missiles. These built in the USA, Germany, China and Japan with designs provided by India. The engines and Laser guns would also be made in India and shipped to the assembly areas.

Ground forces of all countries were supplied with the powerful ground to air Laser canon. The USA and Russia would have submarines around the world equipped with long-range nuclear missiles. There would be more than 100 submarines carrying ten missiles each. The range of these had to be extended but would still have limited range. To take care of this large orbital platforms would be built that would carry nuclear missiles controlled from the ground. Four such platforms would be constructed and would orbit earth

We were not sure that there was time enough to have all this. It would take two years to build 200 space fighters and, at least, three years to build the 20 battleships. One optimistic view was that the aliens had just rebuilt their planet hence may not be able to prepare for an attack on Earth so quickly.

Our India that had been happy so far was now apprehensive and full of fear. The era of peace was coming to an end.

CHAPTER 24

Fear Unites

There was fear everywhere, also anger and a resolve. The world was now clear that it would have to fight for its survival and unite against an enemy who did not care about our country or religion. There were demands that the aliens in India be banished. We explained to the world if these aliens had been hostile they could have enslaved the planet when they first landed. They had also helped us prepare for our defence by giving us the technology to build the Battleships and the space fighters and the force fields for them.

Eleven out our group of thirteen volunteered to join the government panel that was coordinating with other nations for building the planetary defence hardware. Some of them would have to sacrifice their businesses, was the guidance from the masters.

Also, to my IED duties, I was assigned the task of building civilian shelters. We also had to make sure that energy power plants and water storage and pumping facilities put into reinforced underground areas.

I was happy that the TA's had such a large sphere of influence and was sure that they had done something to prevent widespread panic. Despite that people wanted to prepare for the next invasion and this was leading to people hoarding essential commodities. Those who could buy bought ten times more than they needed. The situation prompted some unscrupulous traders to start hoarding. Artificial scarcity created, the prices started spiralling upwards. The poor section of society India, the daily wagers, was hit hard and they started protesting. Government food stocks were released but those too were cornered by hoarders.

The police were hard pressed dealing with riots and was doing anything about hoarders. It was inevitable that the IED was called in. I set up a task force within the department to find out and deal with the problem. Our network of informers got into motion and soon we had identified locations where these hoarded stocks stored. Instead of carrying out raids immediately, we kept watch on the sites and started investigations to find out the person or persons responsible.

Similar problems were being faced by other countries too. They were also finding it hard to find out who was responsible. There was a temptation to carry out raids in the places where these stocks were stored. It was decided to wait for another fifteen days for instigating teams to come up with something.

Another development that was alarming was that even medicines got hoarded. It was happening with dry fruit and tinned stuff too. Some action was needed fast.

The first serious step was taken by the parliament that passed a particular ordinance that those responsible for hoarding of any kind would be executed. The result of this was that there were more stocks available in the market.

The breakthrough came through information provided by one of our group of thirteen. Kavita gave me a call one day and said breathlessly, "Anil I know who is behind the hoarding. I cannot speak on the phone. Can you meet me in Mumbai immediately?" I told her that I would take the next flight to Mumbai. I was picked up by my senior man in Mumbai and reached Kavitas flat. She opened the door and looked terrified. "Anil, the people behind this, is a cartel of very powerful people," she said, "they are some very well connected businessmen and politicians and quite ruthless." I asked her to tell me who they were and she did. Some of them were well known and I was sure that there was someone else very powerful who was behind them. "Why are you so frightened? Kavita." I asked. "They know that I have found out, the wife of one of these people is a friend and she told me. I have not heard from her since then and I am worried" Kavita said.

I assured her that we would provide protection and lady agent from the IED was assigned to her full-time. I also arranged her place to be guarded. I returned to Delhi at once and went to the PM office directly from the airport. I managed to meet with the PM after a wait of an hour.

After the briefing, I was asked to wait. The PM said "We will raid and confiscate all the hoarded material. These will become a part of the governments' emergency stock. I am issuing a warning to members of the cartel and that should make them stop. If they don't, we will take the penal action.

The names of the cartel members are not to be revealed." I did not argue with him and kept quiet.

In the next few days, the raid was carried out and the stocks were moved to government warehouses.

During the following weeks, two cartel members were killed while travelling together in a car accident. Two had a heart attack and another fell down the stair case. Our PM was being ruthless or the person behind the cartel was protecting himself.

The accidents made me very uneasy and during the next meeting of the EID trio I managed to get some time alone with the PM and asked him if he was aware of what happened to the members of the cartel. His reply was strange "It is not only countries that are getting united in times like these" he said. "As you are aware, this hoarding has been happening in every country and the ring leaders everywhere have met the same fate." "The US government has requested us to keep this matter under the wraps. Some families have always profited from war but this time, the world cannot let them get away with it. They are a force that has always worked in the background and they had lost control ever since the aliens came to India. They have always profited from war because they controlled the weapons and oil industries. Oil became valueless with the advent of alien energy technology. They do not get to earn from the spacecraft programme. So they made profiteering on food and other essentials a new way to maintain their control. They had the potential to create a lot of mischiefs. There is no direct or legal way of dealing with them so, in a collaborative effort, all such people have been eliminated."

Tough times require tough measures; I thought and closed this matter in my mind. I had always believed that man is his own enemy and resolved to be more vigilant and keep my team on its toes. I also understood why the guides wanted our people to keep an eye on things. The masters kept watch from another plane and needed people to act on their behalf when required. They had continued their interference minimal so far.

Almost two years had passed. The production of the space fighters and battleships was on schedule. Enough missiles had been produced and dispersal of the submarines around the world had already been dome. The space platforms had taken position around the globe. They were formidable fortresses in the air, bristling with laser canon, conventional missiles, nuclear weapons and crew that could sustain itself for one year, with the supplies on board. Crews were rotated every six months. The battleships were deployed as soon as their trials carried out and all twenty of them were in their positions according to the space defence plan. The space fighters were ready in their stations scattered in ten locations all over the globe.

Ground forces of every country were doubled and stationed in hidden bunkers in bases located near areas identified as potential for an alien landing. Each zone was enclosed by a force field and had enough air troop carriers for redeployment to a sector within a thousand kilometres from each base.

The world was as prepared for the invasion as it could be. The fear of most planners was not so much of the aliens but the fall out of so many nuclear explosions on earth. The plan was to have the nukes explode far outside the atmosphere and use conventional weapons inside it. But the fear was that we may be forced to use these nuclear devices inside the Earth atmosphere if it became necessary.

Another significant concern was that the aliens may also bring in nuclear devices or weapons stronger than they had used so far. According to our Scout-guides they had no such weapons but what we had to fear was their atmosphere destroying devices. If they dropped them, Earth had no defence that could counter it.

The battle plan was that the enemy was not to be allowed be get inside the orbit of the moon. With this in mind, the manufacture of battleships continued and so did the production of space fighters. A big base was also set up on the moon. This base had weapons from where Earth could also be defended. Eight more battle platforms were in various stages of readiness. These would circle the earth at higher orbits and form an outer layer of defence.

We had added two more mining space vessels. These would be able to mine and bring in many minerals from nearby planets. In the last one year, there had brought in one load each. They would continue their operations until stopped by the invasion.

The people of the earth waited. Life went on for the ordinary man and the threat receded into the background. The world had recovered from the last battle. There was talk about colonies that would be set up on other planets and the opportunities that would open up. The prophets of doom preached the end of the world.

On my home front, Mansi expressed a desire to adopt a child. My mother was thrilled and I was sad, I wished she had wanted a child earlier; we could have had one of our own. We would wait until a good child was identified. You can't always get what you want; I hummed the old rolling stones song.

CHAPTER 25

The Wait

Another six months passed. I noticed a rise in crime, mostly murder cases. It was a sign that things were becoming normal. War usually brings down crime. At least, it had done so during the invasion and the period after.

Our preparations for the impending invasion were complete but production of space fighters continued. We wanted as much equipment as we could have to defend our self. I and other officials fine-tuned our safeguards for the civilian population.

Mansi and the other TA's and their more than a million followers volunteered to be a part of the civil defence force. They took on the job of maintaining order at the civilian shelters.

There was some concern about the aliens on Earth. There were some protests by people and even I had expressed concerns to Kishore and also to the PM in our meetings. When I shared my concerns with Mansi, she said that the local aliens would never go against us. I wondered if that is what she felt or it was the indoctrination through the bio-implants that was speaking.

When the PM shared these concerns with the scout-ambassadors, they said that there was always a possibility of rebellion among the aliens and they were very alert to forestall any such thing. To help us deal with any attempt by any rebels to come out of the domes they provided us with detection devices. Only the scout-ambassadors would be allowed to get out of the domes.

The security around the walls of the domes strengthened. I personally supervised the security around the domes. A double ring of barbed wire fencing was put around the walls. These were electrified and had special sensors to detect anything that came within one meter of the fence. Air defence missile batteries laser canon protected the domes from any attempts to breach the walls. My inspection after the installation of the fences and security devices gave my mind some rest.

The time for the attack was coming closer and months passed with nothing happening. I was among those few optimists who hoped that they aliens had dropped their plans to invade. Most people felt that the aliens may be taking time to assemble a stronger fleet. It was this viewpoint that prevailed and production of space fighters was increased. A huge battle cruiser was under assembly at the facility on the moon. Moon based missile batteries were stocked with more nuclear missiles. The moon-based was made stronger. The base was deep underground with strong concrete fortifications and all this was enclosed by a force field. The missile range from the moon was higher and this would be useful to attack the enemy while he was too far from Earth-based missiles.

I got my first opportunity for travelling to the moon. I was asked to go to the moon and inspect the moon base. The PM was keen that find out if there was any security weakness that I could find. I was taken one morning to one of the space fighter bases near Delhi. When I got out of my car I had my first opportunity to see a space fighter from so close. It was one of the space fighters designed on earth fitted with the alien technology engines. It looked like a beetle with a shiny black body, nothing like any aircraft I had ever seen. It was around 120 meters long and 30 meters high, the width seemed to be 30 meters. The nose was transparent. The spacecraft was perched on a circular rubber like cradle on the ground.

When I approached the craft, a door by the side and a ladder folded out. I climbed up and went in. The inside was oval shaped with two seats in front for the pilot and co-pilot. There were two gun positions on the right, two on the left and two behind. As I looked at the pilot came and introduced himself. "Welcome to our spacecraft sir, I am squadron leader Maini. Let me acquaint you with my fighter" He said. He pointed to the gun positions. "There are two guns in the front and missile ports on all sides. The co-pilot doubles as the gunner and controls the front weapons too. The other gunners control the laser cannon and the missile on their sides. We carry conventional missiles as well as nuclear missiles. We have gun positions on top and the bottom too. We have detection systems that feed our helmets as well as monitors on all sides. We have a 360 degree view and can detect anything within 500 km. We carry a crew of nine. " He pressed button and a cylinder slid down. "That is the upper gunners' seat" he said. He pressed another button which opened a circular aperture which leads to the lower gun position. The pilot and co-pilot controlled communication and navigation and the ninth crew member handle medical emergencies. There were four extra seats in the middle for passengers. The seats could be removed if any additional supplies had to be carried. This space fighter used a fuel similar to what all alien engines used and could fly for three months without refuelling. There were enough rations to last for the same period. Water and air were recycled. It was structurally very strong and would withstand a direct hit from an armour piercing shell. It also had a force field. A formidable, solid spacecraft built with the help of our friendly aliens.

We were carrying a full crew and soon as they joined us we floated off. That is the only way to describe the sensation I felt. The craft rose slowly, perhaps because I would not be able to stand a faster take off. Soon we were high above the atmosphere. I was allowed to take the co-pilot's seat a rare honour since I was a first-time space traveller. The sight of the earth below was breathtaking. The moon seen above was shining with a brilliance that was dazzling. The fighter turned and now I could only see the moon.

"There are two bases on the moon. One of them is earthside and one on the dark side. One each is planned on the poles." He explained. I went back to a passenger seat and asked to sleep and told that I would be woken up when we arrived. The journey to the moon orbit would take 24 hours. The weightlessness and being strapped in with an X-harness was initially uncomfortable until I was asked to swallow a pill. I soon dozed off.

The next thing I remember was a loud voice on the intercom on my seat announcing that we were approaching moon orbit. The fighter descended swiftly and soon we were docked at the spaceport of the moon base. I exited the fighter through the door and found a reception committee of two people. In the small gravity of the moon each of my steps was like a jump until I got used to the gravity here.

I was in a small chamber that must have been the size of my bedroom at home. It was brightly lit and the walls and ceiling were painted to resemble a garden. The two persons were the base commander and the base security officer. A door in the wall opened and we entered an elevator which descended fast. "We are a hundred metres underground and the walls above are reinforced concrete. We have three hundred people here to man monitoring stations, laser guns, and nuclear missiles. There are twenty-five space fighters and their personnel housed here. We have medical staff to man our small hospital; we also have a cafeteria and a recreation area."

"We have fifty nuclear missiles and the laser cannon stationed in concrete bunkers spread around the moon. All of them on this side of the moon are controlled from here. In peace time, the station personnel are rotated once in six months and the supplies and water are also restocked. If an urgent evacuation of personnel is required, we send out one of our space fighters". When I asked about the security, I was told that all WSD (World Space Defenders) were embedded with biometric sensors and no one could enter or exit the base without the sensor. If a visitor without one was to be allowed inside, he or she had to be accompanied by two armed personnel from the moon base.

The WSD as a separate entity was formed soon after the first alien attack and would command all space forces, including the space platforms and the moon bases and all battleships and space fighters. The WSD was under the command of the supreme commander of the Earth defence forces.

The hangars for the spacecraft were a hundred metres away from the rest of the base and equally reinforced. There was an underground tunnel connecting the two areas. The missile launchers and their store of missiles were also scattered at a distance. Each could be controlled centrally or from the launcher. There were cameras everywhere monitored by the security chief and his staff.

The base had a deep space monitoring and scanning system that could detect any intruder from a distance beyond Uranus. Its computer would sound the alarm on the base as well as all the WSD sites on earth where space fighters were stationed on earth. I saw a demonstration of this when an intruder alert was sounded. The system had detected approaching fast. When they zoomed in, they found that it was only a large asteroid.

I stayed at each moon base for two days and took the return journey feeling more than satisfied with their security measures. I was also confident that we had a strong base from where earth could be defended. Seeing our planet was a profound experience for me. I was deeply moved and I could not explain why.

I returned to find a worried Mansi waiting for me. It was my first moon trip after all and she was worried about me. It was a great reunion even though it was such a short trip. She sensed a change in me and asked if there was anything wrong. I could not explain why I was feeling so moved. I was feeling a lot of love for her and I expressed it in more than words. Later she wanted details about my trip and was jubilant when I told her that we had such an active defence system based on the moon.

I reported my findings to the chief and resumed my duties here. The PMs' office issued a press release about the moon base and its capability to defend our planet. The news channels picked up the story and this went a long way in reassuring the population. Now there was no fear of terrorists or attacks from other countries. Only the aliens were on everyone's mind.

Every night when I retired I wondered if this night was the night when the alien attack would come. I had nightmares of the Earth being overrun by the aliens and all of us being used as slave labour in their mining camps on far-flung planets. My wife, Mansi had no such fears and kept reassuring me that we would win if we were attacked.

Our prime minister was clear that development must go hand in hand with the defence preparations. He decided that we should adopt countries in Africa and start agricultural production there. Many Indian farmers established huge farms there. Indian industries were also encouraged to set up plants there. The thinking was clear. War may come but we would use every day of peace to build a better and stronger India. Our contribution was making the planet a better place.

In fact, the world had started thinking more about the whole world rather than just countries. With the coming of the aliens, it was clear that much could be gained by finding planets that could be exploited for their resources. If suitable planets were found, we might even be able to shift our growing population to such planets. This thinking allowed for some amount of funds to be allocated to space exploration. Otherwise, defence was going to take it all. Both our mining spaceship had left to find new planets suitable for mining.

The local aliens were becoming more cooperative and gave us more technology. We got the technology for the teleportation devices and improved on it. It worked both ways now but was not yet perfect. The devices worked between two fixed points but not between moving objects. Some exotic material was now used to make better body armour, far better than was available so far.

The aliens still maintained contact with us only through the scout-ambassadors. We were curious if the aliens on Earth had any communication with the home planet and if they had any idea of what was happening over there. Perhaps they had some indications about their invasion plans. Unfortunately, the home planet had blocked all communication with their earth based brethren. The feeling of the aliens on Earth was that they would not be spared during the next invasion. They would now be considered the enemy of their home planet.

The guardians were silent and none of the thirteen was hearing from them. I wondered why they were abandoning us. Perhaps they were being instructed by powers higher than them. It was either that or the guardians had nothing to contribute or communicate at this time.

Suresh Kumar was getting old and he wanted someone to carry on his agenda, someone who could be trusted with his secret pact with the aliens. It had to be someone who would have the interest of the nation most important. It was easy for someone to let power corrupt and he wanted someone who would not be corrupted. At this time, the future of the world depended upon the leader of India.

What he decided had an impact on my personal life. The PM had always wanted to groom his elder son but the son was more interested in expanding his business empire. He was now the world's largest manufacturer of alien technology based energy generators. He had showed no political ambitions and wanted to enjoy his success and money. Suresh, the PM had no choice but to look outside his family. He wanted someone who had a bio-implant and had a large circle of influence and he found that person. My wife Mansi was his choice.

One morning as I was getting ready for work, I got a call from the PM office. The PM wanted a meeting with me and asked me to bring Mansi along. He got to the point at once and said: "I am looking to groom a successor and have chosen Mansi, Anil will you support my decision?". Mansis' face lit up with a smile and I knew that "yes" was the only answer. My mind was in turmoil about this development, because of its implications for our personal life. I was also happy that Mansi had been chosen for this great task. She was going to be a part of events that would go down in history.

Mansi was already a member of the party and was now inducted as an aide to the PM. She would work with him and learn the ropes and when the time came, she would stand for elections. They were three years away unless the alien invasion put it on hold.

Everyone went about their business. I was busy with my responsibilities and Mansi was spending all the time she could getting ready for her future role. All the members of our Guardian followers were busy with the task of overseeing the projects which had been assigned to them.

Another new year dawned and the world celebrated. Some because they thought that the world would end and they should enjoy the time they had. Others celebrated because the aliens had not invaded. People in official positions scanned the skies with apprehension and found it hard to join the celebrations. The scout-ambassadors watched the humans having fun and missed their home planet, wondering when they could live in the open outside their dome prisons.

At the HQ of the planetary defence force, people were busy with simulated alien attacks. Different scenarios were rehearsed. There were a few situations that we were not yet equipped to handle. Everyone here was grateful that there was time for plugging those loopholes. If we had enough time, we would be confident of a victory. At this time, the chances were about 80%. Twenty percent margin for failure was dangerous. Everyone was praying for more time.

The world somehow was a happier. It was like everyone wanted to take as much happiness as they could during this time of peace. No was certain if we would have a life like this anymore. It was the same everywhere, I and Mansi used every little moment with each other to be happy. Every evening when we in town, we went through our list of things we wanted to do together and did them.

Another six months passed. The campaign for the coming elections was being readied. Sureshs' party was beginning to recognise Mansi as the emerging leader. She would be given a ticket for the next election. She and her other TA's and their more than a million followers were busy expanding her sphere of influence. Her name was becoming popular.

Opportunities for us to be together were becoming less and I had to resort to planning my inspection trips so that we were in the same city at the same time, this was better than not meeting at all. I sometimes wondered if all this progress that we had made with the help of the aliens was worth it. If they had not come this terrible situation would not have come to pass. India had let the aliens in and the whole world would suffer for it. However, my meeting with Mansi would not have happened if she had not been abducted.

By time Diwali (an important festival in India) came there still was no sign of the invaders and we had the best celebration in years. The HQ of the planetary defence force had good news for all governments. The simulations predicted a 90% chance of repulsing the aliens.

The next meeting of world leaders was held to discuss the situation. It was felt that if the aliens persisted in their offensive behaviour, we would have to take the war to them. Before that, we would request the local aliens to parley with them. Some felt that we should not do this now because it may look like a sign of weakness and would make sure that the aliens would attack. The decision was taken to boost our military strength and be prepared to invade the aliens.

The preparations were developing the capacity to attack the alien home planet was going well. The aliens had agreed to help us and they gave us the designs for the manufacture of warp drives that were needed to reach Zothar fast. Construction of a base of Mars was begun just after the last attack. The assembly of ten colossal battleships with warp drives was underway and completed in another year or two. Each of these would carry 50 space fighters and 5000 troops. These would be stationed on Mars and an attack on Zothar would be launched at the right time.

Everyone hoped that the world would be able to celebrate Christmas in peace and no alien attack would come.

CHAPTER 26

The Aliens on Earth

We the Zotharians left on earth felt like prisoners of our domes. There were those amongst us who wanted to collaborate with the earth people to find a planet for us where we could finally settle down. Others felt that Earth was the planet we had found for this purpose and we should fulfil this goal, this meant terraforming the planet and would destroy life on earth as it was now. If that happened, the humans would have to live in domes. The other option was to go back to our planet, this was not yet possible.

We knew that the invasion was imminent and would decide about the future based on the outcome of the war ahead. If Zotharians won the battle, every one of us on earth would be executed. If they lost, there was a possibility of doing joint space exploration and finding a planet for themselves.

There was a fear that the earth people may vent their anger on us if our bio-implants failed. The leaders decided that the only thing we should do was to support the earth people to be secure and win the battle, his was the reason that we had helped the earth people with the development of space fighters, battleships and weapons. It was a little time consuming because we could only communicate through the scout-ambassadors.

The earth people were good at adapting our technology and had improved upon many things. Their thinking was not limited to pyramid shapes and the craft they developed looked quite weird to us. The earth people had "nuclear" weapons for which Zotharians had no defence. This technology was scary and had the capacity to destroy this planet. The earth people were requested not to use them inside the earth' atmosphere.

During the first attack on earth, the earth people had to use these "nuclear" weapons to destroy the Zothar landings. It was a necessity and we did not protest. There was relief among us when our aggressive brethren got defeated. Our lives were safe for now.

Now there was fear among us because there was certain to be another attack and this one would be more ferocious. The earth people were warned and asked to step up their preparations. Our little contact with the home planet told us that the attack would take at least three earth years.

There was a possibility that the Zothar would come prepared to deal with this new nuclear weapon that they had faced. Our aggressive brothers may even develop new weapons and there was no way to know this or to warn the earth people about it.

Our stay here in the land was comfortable except for the limitation to stay inside the domes. Many of us got engaged with manufacturing weapons and engines for the space fighters and battleships pf the earth people. Others were busy with the processing of the earth grasses to make our atmosphere and food stuff. Many of us spent out time watching the antics of the earth people on the "TV" programmes that they broadcast.

One good thing was that there was that our population had increased by only 1000. The rate of growth was slightly slower than that on the home planet; this was good because the domes did not get crowded.

We approved of the earth people plan to invade Zothar, this would happen if Zothar attacked again. We hoped that most of the home fleet would be attacking Earth and this may perhaps allow the earth peoples attack to succeed. If they succeeded, we would have a chance to return home.

In the meantime, the earth people were making sure that we had enough food supplies and the material to replenish our atmosphere here. There was enough ORC and other minerals stored here to trade with the humans. In our ten domes on earth, we had six battleships, each with twenty-five space fighters. We would use them if our survival were at stake. The invasion would be as dangerous for us as it would be for the humans. We had to make sure that the humans won the war.

CHAPTER 27

The Shiva Squad

We had been patrolling the area just beyond Jupiter. The Siva squad was one of the 15 space fighters in the area. The rest of the crew and I were the veterans of the fleet. I was getting weary of the endless space. We had already been out for the last one year and except for some relief abroad the battleship the routine was killing.

We docked, with the battleship to replenish our supplies and also stretch our legs a little. We had three days to do both. After a quick shower, I put on a new turban and uniform and went down to the officer's mess. I got myself a drink and was relaxing sitting there enjoying the music. I must have been in a reverie because I suddenly realised that someone was talking, addressing me in chaste Punjabi; this was a pleasant surprise not only because of the language but also because the person talking to me was a girl. Seeing her senior rank, I quickly stood up. "Keep sitting Sardarji", she said and sat down. "Good to meet another Sikh here, very rare to see a turban in the force.

I see you are also an old veteran like me. I joined the force when the first battleship assembled on Earth and now I am the Captain of this battleship." She smiled as she said this.

My medal was the one given to those who fought the aliens during the first invasion. I was also wearing my new rank. The Shiva squad had all been promoted and we were now Lt.Cdrs. I saw the most beautiful girl in front of me and was sorry that she was a senior. It was the first time I had felt so strongly attracted to anyone. She ordered lunch for both of us and we continued to chat while we ate. "My name is Pinky Gill and I am from Jullundur, where are you from?" I told her that I was from Ludhiana, which is just one hour away from her city. We discovered that we had a lot in common except that she was more assertive and bold.

After lunch, she took my hand and said "I like you and can sense that you do too. Come with me." She said and leading the way to her cabin. I followed and soon found myself in a cabin, a first time for me to be in a Captain's cabin. Seeing my nervousness, she said "Relax buddy, nothing bad will happen. I like you and you like me and that is all that matters. Screw the rules and our middle-class morality. Who knows what will happen tomorrow?" I then threw caution to the wind and did what was inevitable in this situation. I was surprised that there was no guilt and only exhilaration. All three days on the ship were spent together and when we parted we exchanged contact details and agreed to get in touch with each other after the war.

My squad mates were surprised about my "disappearance" and also the dreamy look on my face. They could guess that I had

had a tryst with someone but kept ribbing me about that. They wanted me to tell them who it was but I kept mum.

Two months after the restocking there was a ping on the monitors and we spotted an enemy fleet emerging in our sector. "Sound the alarm" I shouted but this was unnecessary because all 50 space fighters had seen the enemy and communicated this to Fleet HQ.

This was the second time we would encounter the enemy and the "Shiva squad" was ready. This time, we were not afraid of the enemy. We had drilled this on simulated battle scenarios and all 50 broke into the three formations one on each side and one behind the enemy. The plan was to let them go ahead with us shadowing them from the flanks and nipping at them from behind.

We had the opportunity to deploy our nuclear missiles before they got close to our fleet and so we got permission to launch an attack. My squad and I were in the fighters behind the enemy and we started closing in. "Let us give it to them, guys. Let us focus on the big beast behind. Four of you take care of any space fighters they deploy and we will go for the big one." I said.

I was piloting the craft today and Renu was the co-pilot and front gunner. As we zoomed in, an enemy space fighter group of 50 fighters headed towards us. The ten of us called in the forty other fighters from the flank so we had fifty of our fighters attacking their fifty from three sides. The enemy had to split to meet the threat and this allowed Shiva squad to get closer to the enemy battleship. We were soon spotted and attacked by three of the enemy. I had to do some slick manoeuvres to avoid getting hit. Our gunners kept pounding away and hit one fighter repeatedly and it exploded.

The swarm slightly behind us was kept busy by our fighters. Two more enemy space fighters exploded. Now they were down to 17 and there were whoops of joy heard on the radio. "I am going in now, guys," I said and reached a point where we could launch our missiles. Just as Renu was about to launch, we were hit twice in succession. There is no way to describe how it feels to be hit by a laser cannon. Unlike the movies, there is no sound just a sudden thud like someone punching you in the gut. The complete fighter vibrated and the temperature inside became hot. I heard Jaya give a shout of joy; she had hit the opponent that had hit us and it was peeling off with debris showering behind it.

We had to hit the battleship before we were crippled. Renu fired two regular missiles and a nuclear missile. I could see them streaking away as I took evasive action to evade the fighters that were still on to us from behind and below. My attention was on that so I did not see the missiles as they streaked towards the enemy. Two our missiles got intercepted but the third sped towards the enemy. Before I could order another salvo, I saw a flash on the video screen. The nuclear missile had got through and the enemy battleship got blown to smithereens.

We had lost twelve out of our fifty fighters but by now our space fighter pilots had a better understanding of the enemy and were confident and more resolute. Our confidence grew when we saw that our battleships had destroyed another enemy battleship.

After this initial hit, the enemy space fighters put a thick shield around their battleships. It would be suicidal for us to attack them now. We had crossed Mars by this time. We got orders to engage the enemy with all our firepower and deplete the size of the enemy space fighters. So we kept fighting them. We were instructed to keep our losses to a minimum but still lost more our space fighters to destroy another fifteen enemy spacecraft.

In our Shiva squad, we were elated because we had destroyed an enemy battleship and four space fighters. All of us were infuriated because of the overwhelming odds and scared that the enemy may manage to land on our planet. The girls had tears in their eyes and I was not sure if it was the rage that was being this way. "There is a long battle ahead. How are we for missile stocks?" I said. "We are down to ten regular and five nuclear, the laser canons will last for at least a month at this rate. If we survive till then" said Renu. "Don't worry Renu we will survive this one too, we are the Shiva squad." I said and there were cheers from the whole crew.

The enemy armada was now approaching the outer ring of the defence platforms and I could see the fierce defence they mounted even though swarms of enemy space fighters attacked them from all sides. They destroyed two alien battleships and many fighters before going down.

There was sadness abroad our ship but satisfaction too. Every enemy downed meant one less for us to confront and defeat. Soon the battle reached the moon base at which point we were ordered to move earth side to assist the defence from there. The moon which unleashed its missile batteries and it was a sight to see. Missiles were streaking out, laser cannon from the moon base flashing and hitting enemy fighters with flashes indicating fighters lost.

The moon bases were getting a pounding but holding. They were deep in the moon and it was hard for the aliens to inflict damage to the facility. They were, however destroying the canon sites and missile launchers. We could soon see the number of missiles rising from the moon diminish.

The enemy was now fully engaged in breaking through our defences and land on earth. All of us attacked as per laid down plans. I looked at the battleships assigned to our group of fighters. There were nine out of which our pack of ten took on one. "Renu, prepare to deploy the standard nukes first and when I give the word fire the nuke," I said. "Group, here we go," I said and went straight to the battleship, ignoring the fighters and letting the others deal with them.

We were hit again and again and heating up but we made it to a point where we could launch. "Now Renu, shoot the standard," I said and she complied. As the ship tried to intercept them, we fired and two missiles, one standard and the other nuke. Two of them went in and we turned away to escape the debris that would soon come our way.

The battle for our planet continued and we kept fighting drenched in our sweat, in our ship that was getting hotter each time we got hit.

CHAPTER 28

The Fight For Survival

Winter was just ending in Delhi and it was nice picnic weather. Mansi and I were planning to go on a holiday; this got put off because the alarm sounded on the thirteen of March. The alien ships got spotted by the monitoring stations on the moon. The public was warned through radio and TV broadcasts immediately. There was fear among the public but no panic because full details of the enemy fleet were not revealed.

The alien ships had suddenly appeared just beyond Jupiter and were moving fast. We had the foresight to station battleships just beyond Jupiter and they formed the first line of defence. We had 15 of them on patrol in the area.

30 alien battleships were approaching accompanied by a swarm of space fighters. Ten more warships of our fleet were ordered to reach that area, leaving 15 behind to defend against

the enemy ships that may get through. 50 space fighters that were already patrolling the area started attacking the aliens.

On Earth, citizens did not panic. People were asked to be ready to move to the shelters. All Earth defences were on full alert. Additional supplies and missiles were rushed to the moon bases because a prolonged battle was likely. Two supply ships that had always been on standby got despatched. They would deliver their stocks long before the aliens reached the moon.

A lot of people were on the rooftops trying to see something, not willing to acknowledge the fact that the battle was too far for anything to be visible from Earth The markets were full of people making last minute purchases of provisions. Enterprising companies were offering special "survival" packs with packaged food and water and essential medicines. Each pack had rations for ten days. There was no shortage even though some people bought two boxes each. More than that would not be allowed into the shelters. TV stations were beaming scenes that the situation rooms were feeding them.

All the shelters were ready to take in people at short notice. Drills had been carried out before so no panic set in. Underground communication networks buried deep connected the shelters to government control rooms. All other installations got plugged in the same way. The moment the aliens crossed Mars all civilians would go to the underground shelters.

The cities became dark as citizens were advised to switch on essential lights only. We did not want our cities to be shining beacons. Police patrolling intensified and unnecessary movement outside homes was discouraged at night time.

Mansi and I moved to the shelter reserved for the highest officials and their families. These were connected to the control bunkers and located in secret locations. We were now ready for the fight. We wondered why we had been moved to the shelters so soon because the enemy would take at least ten days before they reached the moon.

All officials assembled in front of monitors that mirrored those in the HQ of the unified Earth command. The leadership of every country had a situation room just like this. We could see views from the command ship which was the massive battle cruiser we had assembled on the moon. Three-dimensional viewers were showing red dots for the invaders and green dots for our spacecraft. Big dots represented battleships and small dots were space fighters.

We could see the action unfolding. Our space planes were attacking the enemy battleships and were being engaged by their fighters. The space fighters on our battleships deployed in defensive formations around our battleships. They had instructions to use the nuclear missiles only against the battleships.

A fierce battle raged between the two sides. Two our fighters got shot down and soon one of theirs exploded. Some of our best pilots were leading this attack and the strategy was to slip through the enemy fighters and nuke the battleships. One of them slipped through and deployed two nuclear missiles. One of them got intercepted and one of them got through and exploded against the alien ship's force field. The field held for some time and then there was a flash. The enemy battleship exploded. There was a whoop of joy in the situation room.

I had been abroad one of our space fighters and could imagine the nine crew members in the small craft attacking the enemy. I wondered what it would be like inside one of them during the battle. A lot depended on these brave men in the space fighters. The big battleships would be easier targets if they did not have the most manoeuvrable fighters.

In the situation room, all of us anxiously kept looking at the reports of the battle. All eyes were on how many of our spacecraft had fallen to the enemy, the enemy had larger numbers and this was a real concern. I was happy that the usual blood and gore was not visible. Time stood still in the situation room. We would know the time only when we were called out for refreshments. The PM had to be forced to feed himself. He was not a person who got stressed easily but now his stress was visible.

The enemy armada kept pressing forward. Their battleships engaged ours with their laser canon and the distance allowed the force fields of our ships to hold. Space fighters from both sides continued to battle each other. The aliens kept a formation designed to prevent our nuclear missiles from getting through. They were driving a wedge through our formations. The only reason that our 15 ships were able to hold the larger enemy fleet was our nuclear weapons. We had destroyed as many as 20 of their space fighters but there seemed to be many hundreds of them and 28 battleships still fought and kept pressing forward.

Our reinforcements of ten battleships arrived and swung around to attack the enemy from behind. The enemy was prepared for this and fifteen battleships turned around to engage our battleships. There were now two fierce battles going on in space. In the situation room, we watched the red and green dots swirling around with flashes to indicate exploding ships, this got supplemented by a running report from the Earth HQ control centre.

Our fleet that had attacked from behind fired a salvo of conventional missiles and nuclear missiles. The salvo got directed at one enemy battleship. There were 20 missiles and the enemy could not intercept all. The enemy battleship disintegrated, this strategy was working and got repeated. What was making this difficult was a large number of enemy space fighters who were attacking our fleet and deflecting a lot of our resources.

The opposition was strong and their space fighters outnumbered ours. The enemy fleet was moving forward inexorably and our fleet kept attacking their ships from behind and the flanks, this was a part of the strategy to draw them closer to the moon base while inflicting losses on them. Our outer ring of defence platforms floated between the moon and Mars and would be a barrier that the enemy would have to cross.

As soon as the aliens approached Mars, civilians were moved into the shelters. There were some panic situations but, on the whole, the move to the shelters went peacefully. My operatives were giving me reports and making sure that nothing untoward happened.

By the time the enemy reached the outer layer of our defence platforms just beyond Mars, they had 27 battleships left. The defences of the platforms accounted for another two enemy battleships. These platforms got attacked with a massive force of space fighters and finally succumbed to the vast numbers attacking them. They still managed to destroy 40 enemy fighters. The enemy had 25 battleships by the time they reached the moon base. We had lost more battleships out of the ones deployed near Jupiter and had 18 left.

We saw the moon base defences swing into action. Our battleships and space fighters pursuing the enemy fleet kept up the concentrated attack and depleted the enemy fleet by another five battleships. The enemy advance guard comprised of at least 100 space fighters approached the ring of attack platforms around the earth. The 20 enemy battleships kept engaging our 18 battleships that had followed them and their fighters attacked the moon base. The space fighters from the moon base rose up and engaged them. Another battle ringed the moon. At closer distances, between the enemy and us the deployment of nuclear weapons was sometimes difficult.

Soon we had lost another five battleships and the enemy had lost two. The numbers of space fighters lost were not accurately known. But one thing that we could see on the screens in the situation room was that both sides were losing a lot of fighters. The tension in the situation room was mounting and our spoke for the first time to the command centre. He wanted an assessment but got politely told that a report would follow as soon as the supreme commander was a little less engaged.

Our attack platforms were powerful enough to repulse that enemy space fighter and destroy half of them. The rest were engaged by our fighters deployed from the earth and the moon base. Many of the aliens sneaked through and attacked our land-based military installations. They had very powerful bombs that destroyed two of our installations, one in India and another in China. We had a hundred fighters defending our planet. They prevented more enemy space fighters from breaching our atmosphere.

Each person in the situation got very tense when we saw ten enemy battleships in close formation surrounded by 75 space fighters thrust though our forces and head straight for earth. They seemed to have a combined force shield that was not letting any of our weapons get through. Earth-based nuclear batteries were now brought to bear. A concentrated salvo brought down 35 alien fighters and one battleship. It was good that it was well outside the atmosphere. We would find out later what damage this would do to us. Our reserve of fifteen battleships was brought in and they attacked the remaining nine enemy battleships. The battle raged on.

It was difficult for the earth batteries to target the aliens now as the earth ships were too close to them. The aliens and their support fighters were fighting hard were holding back our fleet. Four enemy battleships were making an attempt to breach our defences and land and it looked like they would get through.

The four battleships and their support fighters entered our atmosphere and once they were inside, they used a strange weapon. They would direct something at an approaching missile or aircraft and emit a whine and this would destroy any craft that approached it. Our conventional anti-aircraft batteries could not penetrate their force fields. Our jet fighters and all missiles fired at it just exploded as they approached.

Out in space, the battle raged on. Our forces saw what was happening on earth and fought desperately. They were able to overwhelm completely the five battleships and destroy them and also all the enemy space fighters. Our forces had to pay a price. We lost eight space platforms and 50 space fighters. The number of our battleships was down to 15. Both the moon bases had received enough damage to prevent most of the missile launchers from firing. Major repairs would be required and work on this had started.

The monitoring stations on the moon were still functioning and were keeping a close watch to detect any reinforcements being sent by the aliens. They had not lost any personnel.

All four of the enemy battleships accompanied by fifteen space fighters landed in a remote location in mid-Africa. Air recon showed that they formed four corners of a vast square and established a defensive perimeter with some vehicles. Soon a dome enclosed this area. Their fifteen space fighters patrolled overhead.

Ground attacks would soon be launched against the invaders but our strategists had many questions that had to be answered before an all-out attack was launched. The first was how we deal with their space fighters with their strange new weapon. The second was how long they would be able to survive on Earth without replenishing supplies. Were they expecting reinforcements to arrive? The local friendly aliens informed us that these invaders could last for at least a year or even more depending upon how many personnel and supplies were on board.

Planetary defence HQ ordered ground-based missile batteries to engage with the space fighters. They took evasive action but did not use the new weapon. Perhaps the weapon could only be used by the battleships. The enemy space fighters evaded the missile attacks with skilful flying. The aliens were waiting for something and our defence forces felt that an immediate attack should be launched.

Our scout-ambassadors had informed us that the aliens could not tolerate bright sunlight so our forces moved in and surrounded the alien dome at noon time. A large number of powerful light arrays were stationed around the dome to keep the enemy at a disadvantage.

There were enough tanks and artillery to keep the aliens inside the domes. What was feared was that if the battleships took off, they would devastate our forces with their strange weapon. What we were not sure of was if they could use the weapon from the ground. An air attack was ordered against the enemy space fighters and this managed to destroy four of the enemy space fighters, we lost fifteen fighter aircraft. It was clear that the strange weapon could not be fired from the ground. With this information, there was hesitation in deploying our space fighters. In a dogfight that lasted for twenty minutes, all enemy space fighters were destroyed.

Ground forces attacked the perimeter defence of the aliens but were repulsed again and again with heavy casualties. Artillery fire would not penetrate the dome but it would diminish enemy fire from the perimeter defence. Our forces kept up the missile and artillery barrage against their perimeter defences.

It was clear to all of us in the situation room that destroying the dome and the four battleships within it was critical, this had to be done quickly before the aliens had time to do whatever they planned.

Our forces in space were kept ready to destroy these ships if they rose out of the atmosphere. Our fleet was depleted and we wondered if we would be able to defend our self if there was another attack. The repair work on the moon was proceeding at a hectic pace and the bases would be ready for action soon. We hoped that the repairs were complete before the next attack came.

The civilian populations had some respite and were allowed out of the shelters. They had not yet been given the news about the developments in Africa. It was common to see people looking at the sky fearfully from time to time. There was a feeling of relief when it was announced that we had won the battle, this was not entirely correct but we had certainly scored a victory of sorts. Only the people in the situation rooms around the world were aware of the crucial battle to destroy the dome in Africa.

There was a feeling in official circles that if the aliens did not attack again for a year or two, we might be able to bolster up our defences. They wondered what would happen if the aliens attacked earlier than that.

The alien attackers had settled inside their dome inside their defence perimeter. Earth Defence HQ ordered our forces to stop firing. The firing stopped and we waited to see what would happen next. It was certain that the aliens were waiting for something.

Our observers could see movement inside. Some machines seemed to be ploughing the earth in the big square inside the dome. The green gas was soon released inside the dome and nothing more could be observed after that.

A video conference of world leaders was called. The world defence force commander gave his report and asked for instructions. He wanted to proceed with the attack and destroy the enemy dome. The leaders conferred and agreed. If there were another attack coming it would not help to have the enemy dome on earth. The alien scout ambassadors also felt the same way but could not help with suggestions to penetrate the alien defences.

Before another attack could be launched at the dome, there was news that another alien Armada had been sighted. There were another 20 alien battleships on their way. They came accompanied by another 100 space fighters. They had crossed Uranus and were expected to reach the moon in ten or twelve days.

The WDF broadcast details about our defence preparations throughout the world, this was obviously done to make our citizens feel safe. The defences on earth unyielding and it would be hard for the aliens to get through our atmosphere through our missile shields. We had ten space platforms that had survived and were placed just beyond the range of our missiles. If the aliens got past them, the earth missile defences would be the next line of defence. We had 15 battleships and

150 space fighters still functioning. So the odds were not so bad except for the four enemy battleships on the ground and the new weapon that was so devastating.

When I got this news, I quickly informed Mansi and then called up others of our group of thirteen. Some of them already knew. Kishore had called them. We now knew that the time had come for us to play our part. The survival of humanity would be soon at stake.

In the situation room, we saw the ground forces quickly withdraw to a safe distance. As soon as that was done the order was given by the defence command to attack. A camera at one of the mobile launch - sites showed us images of missiles streaking towards the enemy dome. We hoped that the flat trajectory flights of the missiles may escape detection and they did. The nuclear explosions ripped into the dome and we could see a huge mushroom cloud. It took a while for the cloud to clear enough for us to see the impact site. Their entire perimeter defence was gone. The dome was broken and inside it three of the pyramid shaped battleships were crumpled and the forth seemed dented but it stood nothing could be seen moving. "We have done it" shouted one of the military officers in the situation room. Everyone was smiling and some were prancing about with happiness.

Images from the site of the battle showed the enemy battleship trying to rise but could not go beyond hundred metres before dropping to the ground. It seemed badly damaged but kept trying to rise only to fall again. Very soon our fighters dropped heavy bombs on it. Its shields must have been disabled because the bombs that dropped on it completely obliterated it.

The PM announced to the room "We had won the battle but the war is not yet over. The deciding factor now would be the space battle with the enemy fleet. The enemy would reach the moon in nine or ten days." The attacking force had more battleships, we had more space fighters plus defences on the moon and also the space platforms. The ace that our PM was holding would attack Zothar at the right time and would perhaps give us an advantage. He was yet willing to let anyone know about this secret force on Mars. Both sides were desperate and would be fighting for the survival of their species.

We were all allowed out of the situation room for a few days. On our way home Mansi and I called my mother to find out if she was alright. When we reached home, Mansi said: "what do you think will happen, Anil?" "It is hard to say, but our boys are good and now that they are familiar with the aliens' way of fighting they will do better." I said. I held her and she sobbed, "We have lost so many space pilots, I wonder how their families must be coping? She kept crying. There was nothing to be said. We decided to make the most of the few days we had together. God alone knew what the future would bring.

The next day I gave a call to my uncle. His son was in the space force and was flying aboard a space fighter. His son was dead and his squad had lost four space fighters, a total of 36 personnel dead. My aunt was so upset that she did not come to the phone. They would not even see their sons' dead body. Bodies of pilots killed in space never came home. Many families around the world had lost sons and daughters. There was a lot of sadness everywhere. Gurjeet was lucky, his son Santhok who was in the Space Force had survived. He had come home for three days while his spacecraft was being serviced and restocked, one of his squad members Jaya had also come with him she had no family to go home to.

"We harboured these aliens and got so much from them and now there was so much bloodshed and destruction. We had put an end to this kind of violence on Earth and now it had returned in a way that we had never imagined." I thought. I wondered how Suresh must be feeling and how the aliens on earth felt. Their survival was also at stake. I wondered if the scout ambassadors had met the PM and what they had to say.

This time outside also gave me the opportunity to speak to the others in the "Guardian" group. We had to be prepared to activate the resistance in case we lost the war; this was a group spread all over the world known only to a select group of officials in each government. They would fight against the aliens when required.

The heads of state reviewed the situation with the Commander in Chief. He was confident that we could win with our new knowledge of the enemy's moves. The only thing that made the outcome uncertain was the new weapon that the enemy had started using.

The question on everyone's mind was "Are we going to be annihilated?"

CHAPTER 29

The Invasion Fleet

Deep inside the Mars base, the invasion Fleet waited. Admiral Kaushal Singh, Commander of the Fleet, waited impatiently. He was waiting for the Zotharian invaders to reach the Earth-Moon. When the alien fleet engaged the Earth defences, this invasion fleet would head for Zothar.

Admiral Kaushal reviewed reports from the battleships under his command. All the massive ships carried fifty space fighters each and five thousand soldiers with heavy weaponry. They carried troop landers which could carry one thousand troops. Each ship carried ten medium sized tanks. Every space plane took nuclear weapons as well as conventional arms. Every one of the personnel had a bio-implant and this enabled communication and control

The troops wore armoured spacesuits with oxygen generators. These suits had an air capacity of one week. The troops had special laser rifles that also fired regular bullets. One soldier carried two hundred rounds of ammunition and twenty grenades. Every company had a two heavy laser cannon and handheld missile launchers. Backup ammunition was plentiful.

Kaushal was away from Earth since after the first alien invasion and had built the invasion fleet on this base on Mars. He spent two decades in the Indian air force before his deputation to the Space Force; he had no family just like every man and woman on this base. He was a well-built serious looking person who liked his solitude and his books and music. An orphan, he had been raised in an orphanage until he was old enough to go to a military school. His intelligence and ambition got him into to the Indian Air Force. When the new Space Force got formed, he was deputed to head it.

He had never had time for anything except his career and no family so he was the natural choice for the top secret Mars assignment.

Every person on this mission understood its importance and realised that success meant the survival of humanity. They had planned for every possible situation based on information provided by the Scout Ambassadors. Unexpected situations could not be ruled out.

As soon as the alien fleet had gone beyond Mars, a scout craft sped on its way to Zothar. Its mission was to find out if there were more battleships ready to be launched to attack Earth and also to gauge the Zotharian defences.

The Scout ship spotted one battleship around the planet and a ten space fighters. Our scout returned undetected and took his place with his squadron. The fleet waited for developments on Earth.

The standing orders of the fleet were to attack Zothar with the intention to force the Zotharian fleet to turn back to defend their planet, intercept and destroy the alien fleet.

Our fleet also had the mandate to destroy the hostile population of Zothar and return our peace-loving allies to their planet.

The morale of the personnel on the invasion fleet was great. Each person was confident and had clarity of purpose. A victory was guaranteed.

On board one of the troop landing craft, Colonel Surinder Rathore looked at his battalion with pride. He had fought in the battle on Myanmar where he had served as a Company Commander in the same regiment he commanded now. All his soldiers were in peak physical condition, and they had familiarity with the enemy based on information provided by the Scout Ambassadors.

Earth people moved faster than the aliens and that was a distinct advantage. The disadvantage was the confinement of the spacesuits and unfamiliarity with the terrain. Rathore being a realist had no illusions about what lay ahead. Cleary, what lay ahead was not going to be easy. He and all the invading force had planned for every situation and yet as a commanding officer he knew that unforeseen events always happen on the battlefield. He wondered how many of his troops would survive the coming conflict.

Soon the order was given to proceed towards Zothar and Rathore gathered his company commanders to review the tactics for the last time before they reached Zothar. He clarified once again that no prisoners were taken or any dead or injured left behind under any circumstances.

CHAPTER 30

Zothar Invasion

Earth gave the signal and the fleet zipped off to Zothar. Kaushal and his team surprised the alien battleship on guard in Zothar and destroyed it. The space fighters caused nuisance and soon destroyed.

Kaushal Singh looked at the alien planet shrouded in its green atmosphere and waited for the return of the alien fleet. His scouts had reported locations of populated areas. He was averse to what he had to do but had no choice about destroying the entire population here on orders from his PM.

The strategy of this fleet depended on the number of battleships that returned to confront them. Earth soon signalled that five alien battleships and an unknown number of space fighters had been spotted heading back.

Kaushal ordered the attack on the alien planet. Fifty space fighters accompanied the landing craft carrying troops to the landing zones. The planet had five population centres he had orders to destroy them..

What happens next?

The saga will continue. Wait for the sequel to this book and find out what happens in the final battle and after it ends. Will earth and its people survive? What will happen to the friendly aliens on earth? What role will the guardian group play in times to come?

Printed in the United States
By Bookmasters